KT-227-710

Pistolman

STEVE FRAZEE

Sagebrush
Large Print Westerns

Library of Congress Cataloging in Publication Data

Library of Congress Cataloging in Publication Data was not yet available at the time this book was printed.

Libraries should call (800) 251-8726 and we will fax or mail the CIP Data directly to them.

Cataloguing in Publication Data is available from the British Library and the National Library of Australia.

Copyright © 1952 by Steve Frazee. Copyright © 1967 by Steve Frazee in the British Commonwealth. Copyright renewed 1980 by Steve Frazee. Published by arrangement with Golden West Literary Agency. All rights reserved.

Sagebrush Large Print Westerns are published in the United States and Canada by Thomas T. Beeler, Publisher, Box 659, Hampton Falls, New Hampshire 03844-0659. ISBN 1-57490-161-3

Published in the United Kingdom, Eire, and the Republic of South Africa by Isis Publishing Ltd, 7 Centremead, Osney Mead, Oxford OX2 0ES England. ISBN 0-7531-5948-1

Published in Australia and New Zealand by Australian Large Print Audio & Video Pty Ltd, 17 Mohr Street, Tullamarine, Victoria, 3043, Australia. ISBN 1-86442-261-0

Manufactured in the United States of America by BookCrafters, Inc.

Pistolman

CLAY ARBUCKLE WAS ALONE AGAIN, WITH ONLY THE uneasiness of the last few months huddling against him for company. He thought of coyotes crying into the lostness of night, for that was how he felt.

South Fork was another town, and Dutch Holcomb's Horseshoe saloon another place for Clay to wait for his father to return and say that they would stay a spell in this part of the country below the mountains, or ride on again. Old Jeff and Clay never lit anywhere for long.

Behind them was a long trail, twisting through many places, touching nowhere on a wide spot that marked obligation to other human beings. Now that he was learning to look back with some measure of detachment, Clay realized he had never known a friend.

"You don't need friends," Jeff always said. "That way you got fewer enemies."

There were six men near the other end of the bar. Their conversation lifted in curves of normal intentness and then sank into little silences; but when they talked it was mainly of things Clay knew, of cattle and riding, of grass that grew no longer where it once had been.

Clay felt a bond between him and the others but he knew they would not recognize it if he tried to move into their group. During the last few months, at times when Jeff was absent, Clay had tried to feel his way toward friendship but each time some quality that he seemed to push before his good intentions brought tension to others.

"Friends are enemies with a smile." Jeff had taught his son to study men, to color all their tiny actions with significance, and to trust them not at all. Jeff had taught well, until the habits thus ingrained were a curse.

One of the six men said, "Another blistered year like this—and then what?"

1

It was a self-answering question, apparently, for the others let it stand as such. Most of them looked at their whiskey glasses or at themselves in the mirror; but one was watching Clay. They were small ranchers from the hills west of town, Clay knew by their talk. From habit, he had weighed them individually and as a group, and now he recognized what the coyote calls had caused him to overlook at first: the set face of danger.

Dissatisfaction with the careful pattern of his life was strong in Clay, but the feeling was not rebellion yet; and so he played again the old, cold game Jeff had taught him.

As a rider would study a mean horse, thinking, "Can I ride him?" so Clay had been trained to look at men, asking himself, "Come trouble, which ones are left-siders and which ones are on the right?" Once it had been a game, but now the automatic measuring was as instinctive as hunger.

Perhaps it has marked me in some way, Clay thought.

He made his observations a second time. The gaunt man who had just turned his deep-set eyes away was the real right-sider of the group. On the right were the cold ones; on the left the inept, the afraid, and the over-eager ones. The simple placement came from the days when Jeff set targets on both sides of a sage bush, saying, "The one on the right will kill you if you try to deal with both all in a flurry."

As Clay reckoned, he must have been about twelve when the game started. He had been in it ever since.

Others played the game too. This gaunt man down the bar, whose name was Anse Honeywell, had studied Clay and recognized a fellow player. He was thinking about Clay now, roasting him on a mental spit. It always happens, Clay told himself. He was puzzled because

2

what others saw in him he could not see himself.

Framed between two fluted columns of cherrywood, his face looked out at him from the backbar mirror. It was dark, flat-cheeked. The brows were heavy. The eyes were frank with just a little hooding at the outer corners, which gave the whole expression a sort of wondering look.

"Don't that clock run no more, Dutch?" The voice jumped into a small run of silence.

Clay's vision flicked from his own image to a point on the glass that reflected the face of the speaker. Another Honeywell. This one was Barr Honeywell, and he was a right-sider too, but he did not stand there as sharply defined as the one called Anse. His little movements had not been quite as economical as his brother's, and he lacked the air of deliberate listening silence.

Dutch Holcomb said, "Jess forgot to pull the weights, I guess." Dutch was a beefy man with orange-colored hair lying in tight curls on a narrow skull. His heels bumped on the sanded floor.

He was hurrying too much for a heavy man, in his own place; he was over-anxious to do something with his hands. Clay watched him start toward the clock, and that was all. Six men in town on a dead day, six men waiting. They had been here when Clay entered, but the bottle before them was not hurt much.

Anse Honeywell looked at Clay. "Do you have the time, friend?" His voice was civil, deep.

After a few moments Clay said, "Ten after eleven."

Anse Honeywell eyed the expensive watch. He balanced it against Clay's weather-stained clothing, and against Clay's pistol, an ordinary one worn on the left side in a holster little different from any that the

3

ranchers wore. "Thank you," he said, and turned away.

The clock made long ticks in the room. Suddenly, as if he had been trying not to do so, Dutch looked into the street. Long windows flanking the door were so clean Clay saw the ripples and blue puddles caused by imperfections in the glass.

From where Clay stood, South Fork was a saddle shop, the Comet Cafe, the sheriff's office, and a long-fronted general store with high windows. In a vacant lot next to the store, weeds were scrubby fuzz against the dust. Even the nettles under the eaves drip were small and limp. The street was dead. A heavy sun lay on everything.

Dutch Holcomb came quickly, heavily, across the room, as if his place behind the bar would give security. Both Honeywells and the two men next to them were watching Clay now. A little nudge to call attention . . . a side movement of the eyes to direct it. . . Wherever Clay went it happened to him.

"Did somebody goose you, Dutch?" It was the stocky little man again. "You're jumpy," he said. He could not talk away his own tension.

"I'm all right, Andrews." Dutch glanced at the ranchers' bottle. He dragged his towel along the bar as he walked on up to Clay. "Another one, mister?"

Clay's glass was full. Sometimes he took one drink, not caring for it any more than he liked tobacco. Standing at a bar was an outward sign of being just like any other man, but lately he had been spilling his one drink into a cuspidor before paying for it and walking away.

Dutch blinked at Clay's glass. "I didn't notice."

There were small remarks for such a situation, Clay knew, but he did not know how to say them.

4

One of his first memories of Jeff was his father's saying, "An empty barrel is noisy. Remember that, Clay."

Sweat was sopping into the edge of Dutch's shirt collar. He glanced at the dead street again, and then to Clay's wooden stare he said, "I just didn't notice it was full, I guess." He walked away, stopping between Clay and the ranchers.

"What's the matter, Dutch?" Anse Honeywell asked in his slow, pleasant voice.

Dutch swung around. Clay watched him build anger. He built it almost to the point of letting his temper speak for him, and then the sharp point wilted. Dutch said, "I'm all right, Anse." He began to polish wine glasses.

What was it this time, in this place called South Fork? Men's troubles were their own. Clay knew he should have left the Horseshoe ten minutes ago. Jeff would have taken him out sooner than that; Jeff could smell trouble a mile away, and always avoided it if possible.

Clay poured his drink into the flared mouth of a high spittoon. The Honeywells watched him, and then they glanced at each other. They could not know, Clay thought, that his sudden decision to stay in the Horseshoe had nothing to do with them, except that they were two representatives of a world filled with unfriendly men, so to hell with them.

Clay went to a table against the back wall of the room. There was a hall to his right and on his left a wide entrance to a dance floor. He sat with his chair clear of the table, with his feet squarely under him, and he told himself that he had a right to be here, waiting for his father.

The conversation of the ranchers dwindled to silence. Andrews, the little jumpy man, downed his drink and poured another. Anse Honeywell took the bottle then and shoved it up the bar toward Dutch.

Somewhere in the hall a door opened and banged shut. Dutch nearly dropped a glass before he juggled it onto the backbar. The Honeywells looked toward someone Clay could not see. Barr would have moved away, but his brother touched his arm. Anse shook his head and Barr stepped back in line.

As the footsteps came up the hall Dutch worked his lips nervously and jerked his head in a go-back signal. The woman came into Clay's sight an instant later. She was small, with sand blond hair. She was much too good looking to fall into Jeff's category of women you could trust.

"Dancehall fly-up-the-cricks that've lost all their looks—trust them in and out of their rooms one time. Never the same one twice, remember."

"Get out of here, Bitsy," Dutch said.

She paid him no attention. "Six of you," she said, looking at Anse Honeywell. "Is that enough?" Her voice was rounding full. It struck some chord in Clay, warming interest in him, and then the chord went sour and the lonely coyote cries were ringing in his mind.

Anse Honeywell said, "I think so, Bitsy."

A polite man, Clay thought, with the civility running thinly over an iron coldness.

Barr Honeywell left the bar and started toward the woman. "Now look, Bitsy—"

"Never mind." She saw Clay then and went toward him, leaving Barr in the middle of the room, his tongue quiet but his hand still reaching toward explanation.

"Hello, cowboy." She pulled a chair out and sat down across the table from Clay.

Cowboy. Clay started warming up again; she had

6

taken him for what he considered himself to be.

"I'm Bitsy Miller. I work here."

That did not cover everything. Her smile was natural, and the same quality seemed to run deep inside her. Clay could not say, "Dancehall girl," and let it go at that. That was what Jeff would have done.

Maybe I'm getting tired of what Jeff does, Clay told himself.

He kept staring at the woman. Her eyes were the darkest blue he had ever seen. He did not class her with the dancehall girls he had known, but he knew no other way to approach her, so he asked, "Drink?"

She shook her head. From the corner of her eye she watched Barr Honeywell rejoin the other ranchers. He took a different position, away from his brother, and his eyes laid a challenge before anyone who cared to smile at him for being left in the middle of the floor.

Clay shifted his chair, restoring to sight part of the group that Bitsy's presence had cut from view.

"Are you going to work around here?" she asked.

"Maybe." It sounded harsh to Clay.

Dutch Holcomb said, "You're bothering the man, Bitsy. Why don't you—"

"*I* didn't say so." The words came out so readily Clay wondered at himself.

Only one of the batwings was left wagging when a little man popped through the door. His face was mainly bulging eyes and a purplish nose. "Krimble and old Chaunce in a wagon," he said quickly. "Jim's girl is riding beside the rig."

Anse Honeywell said, "Give him a bottle, Dutch."

"That ain't so good, his girl being along." The rancher was a tremendous, squint-eyed man. He spoke of a girl but he looked at Clay.

7

"Don't get it up in your neck, Callaway." Anse went to a window and the others followed.

Andrews' voice was jerky. "Hey! The sheriff's door just opened, but he didn't come out!"

"So he didn't go to Rosita after all," Anse said. "What of it, Andrews?"

The ranchers looked around at Clay. They thought they were between two fires now. Let them stew! The old fierceness of being apart was like cold awl points touching Clay lightly on the back of the neck. He hated all men at the moment.

"Clear out," he said to Bitsy.

The ranchers watched the woman walk away. They looked at Clay, and then they looked to Anse Honeywell for strength.

Dutch was polishing a glass with the urgency of a badger digging for its life. "Those windows, boys. I hope . . ." He knew he was talking into air.

Anse said, "Barr, you and Andrews in here. The rest of us will step out."

Andrews bit his mustache, looking over his shoulder at Clay. "I don't much like—"

"I see that," Anse said. "All right, do you want Big George to stay with Barr, and you go with us?"

"Something ain't just right," Andrews said. "Ben Wavell is over there, and—"

"Yes or no?" Anse Honeywell asked. He was not impatient or angry. "Do we go through with it?"

"No," Andrews said. "Not this way." He walked to the bar, wiping his palms on his coat.

Quite pleasantly Anse asked, "Who's next? Limberis—you?"

Limberis was a grizzled, rawhide string of a man. He looked at Clay for a moment. "Yeah," he said. "Yeah,

8

Honeywell, I'm next." He joined Andrews at the bar.

Here was a place for laughter, but Clay had never known the feel or sound of it within him. He watched the last two men with the Honeywells shake their heads and walk away. The sheriff's quietly opening door had done part of it, and Clay had done the rest by just sitting at their backs, a threat composed of coldness and silence.

The spotter who had warned the ranchers of the wagon was drinking his reward. Perspiring fat hung over the back of his collar. He had paid no attention to anything but the whiskey.

A light spring wagon and a rider passed the big front windows. Clay saw two men, one black-jowled and heavy; the other a thin, erect old man with a jutting nose. They did not glance toward the Horseshoe. A girl in a divided skirt and bright blue blouse was riding a brockled bay beside the wagon.

She glanced toward the saloon, but the sun was on the windows and she could not have seen inside. She smiled at the black-jowled man and said something. He nodded. Her hair, Clay decided, was about the color of Bitsy's. The wagon went out of sight.

Standing at the end of the bar, Bitsy said, "I'd give my share in the hot place for a figure like that."

"Yours ain't bad." Dutch was all at once a happy man. "A round on the house, boys!"

"Give mine to Andrews and Limberis," Anse Honeywell said. The implication was there, but his voice was even, pleasant. "Come on, Barr."

Barr hesitated at the door. He looked at Clay and then at Bitsy before he followed his brother outside. Clay sat where he was until all the ranchers had left, and then he walked slowly toward the door.

"Come in again, cowboy," Bitsy said.

The wagon was up the street in front of the Range Hotel where Clay was staying. Six men were riding out of town, two in front, four behind in the slow-setting dust of the first pair. Across the street a man was standing in the doorway of the sheriff's office with a rifle at his side.

"Clay Arbuckle?"

The man with the rifle wore a small sheriff's star from which the plating was peeling. His cheeks were pink and full. His eyes were mild, scarcely questioning, although he had just asked a question. Altogether, his face was an innocent blank, puzzling to Clay because it offered nothing for quick classification.

Clay stopped. He nodded.

"Step in, if you're not rushed. I'd like to talk to you. My name is Ben Wavell."

It was not an order, but still there was a pull of authority in the words. Clay stepped inside.

Dodgers tacked on four corners nearly covered one wall of the office, completely corralling a half dozen beer company calendars. Wavell put his rifle in a rack. He sat down and lifted his feet to his desk. He was wearing Congress gaiters.

"Light somewhere and rest a spell," Wavell said.

Clay moved along the front wall to a chair. He put one boot on it and waited. South Fork was an off-trail place for his name to be known; in fact, his name was not well known anywhere, he thought.

"You killed a couple of toughs in Hallidane about six weeks back," Wavell said. "I guess they got what they wanted, from what I heard." He wiggled his toes in his soft shoes and said, almost regretfully, "I used to have their pictures right there over that six-horse team by

10

your shoulder."

The Paynter cousins. They had worried about Clay for an hour there in that Hallidane saloon. Old Jeff had been scouting around the country as usual. At last the Paynters asked Clay flatly what he wanted with them. He did not even know who they were, not then; he had been watching and studying them because he was not quite sure whether they were right-siders, or part bluff.

Damn that deadly habit of sizing up all men!

"You remember the two I'm talking about?" Wavell asked.

Clay nodded. When he told the Paynters he did not know them at all they would not believe him. Maybe they thought he was a lawman. Maybe they just didn't like his looks. Pistol fights could start from less than that.

Jeff had been angry about the trouble when he found out. "Keep it up!" he said. "Then you'll be known."

"The marshal cleared you, didn't he?" Wavell asked.

Clay nodded.

"The law clears lots of things." Wavell clasped his hands on his stomach and pushed his thumbs together. His hands were long and powerful; fingers like his sometimes marked a man in a card game, but the fingers served only a small role in pistol work.

Silence and sharp scrutiny did not bother Wavell. He said, "I never saw the Paynters. I know the Honeywells. Just guessing, I'd say Anse and Barr are some tougher than the Paynter boys ever could have been."

That was probably true, Clay thought.

"How old are you, Arbuckle?"

"I don't know." Clay thought he knew, within a year or so.

"Texas?"

11

Clay did not know where he had been born. The sheriff's tongue was hinged in the middle. "Great talkers are great liars," Jeff said. But Wavell seemed frank and friendly. Some of them tried to pry with a tightness pinching at their eyes, denying what a man would say before the words emerged.

"Oklahoma?" Wavell asked.

Clay shook his head. Not knowing his background made him feel ashamed, so silence was the best answer.

Wavell took no offense. "The Honeywells and the others figured to kill Jim Krimble and his foreman, old Chauncey Wade. Billy Smithers—he lied to me when I came into town. Billy was their lookout. You seen him. They paid him with a bottle, huh?"

"Uh-huh."

"I thought the Honeywells were in there alone." Wavell glanced at his rifle rack. "Otherwise, I would have gone over and taken a hand in things. I don't like any kind of trouble but when it has to be, I like to see it kept fair. Being Krimble's friend, I sort of favor him. Being in the middle, I hope I'm man enough to play it square." Wavell paused. "Just what did you do a minute ago to cool 'em off?"

"Nothing. Just sat."

The sheriff's eyes were mild but not innocent. "That was all, huh?"

"They saw your door open."

"But you were the one with a pistol behind him. Did they know you, Arbuckle?"

"I don't think so."

"You haven't any interest in the fight?"

Clay shook his head.

"Nobody sent for you?"

"Nobody."

12

Wavell nodded. "I don't think so. Probably you saved Jim Krimble's hide." The sheriff shook his head, looking at Clay's pistol. "But he won't like you for it."

"I'm not asking thanks from him."

"Yeah. I can believe that." Wavell looked a long time at Clay. "Do you ever get hound-dog lonesome, Arbuckle?"

Wavell's habit of throwing sudden kinks in the line of talk made Clay wary. *Hound-dog lonesome.*

"No," he said, but the vision of a lean hound padding along its solitary way stuck in his mind; and it was a symbol of the way he had lived.

"I guess I was thinking of how it would be with me, living your way." Wavell shook his head. "I see I was on the wrong foot, thinking that you'd got into the trouble a-purpose. Hope I didn't interrupt your business, Arbuckle."

When Clay was at the door, the sheriff said, "Mind handing me that broom there?"

Clay leaned the broom against the desk. It began to slide sidewise. Wavell caught it carelessly. "Drop in and chew the rag anytime you got nothing to do. I get sort of weary sometimes, sitting here looking at my pictures."

Alone in the tawny sunshine, Clay felt rebellion growing against the duty of going to the hotel to study two men. Tomorrow he might not even be in this country. For a while there in the sheriff's office he had been more interested in a man as an individual than as a potential target to be placed to the left or right.

Instead of going toward the hotel, Clay walked across the street to the Horseshoe. Dutch was polishing the bar vigorously. He was singing, but when he saw Clay the song dwindled away. Bitsy Miller was standing at the window. She smiled.

"You made a quick trip, cowboy."

She couldn't weigh more than a hundred and ten with a rock in each hand. She was as pretty and sharp as a quail. There was something in her frankness that reminded Clay of the sheriff. Knowing no way to make easy conversation, he asked bluntly, "What's the trouble between Krimble and Wade and the other?"

"You don't know?" Bitsy asked.

Dutch spoke up quickly. "I told you Krimble never would hire anyone to help him out of trouble. He's got Texan ideas, Bitsy. I told you all that."

"I know," she said. "But I asked this cowboy." The blue eyes looked at Clay as if she had known him a long time.

"I don't know, or I wouldn't have asked," Clay said.

"It's range," Bitsy said. "Lone Star owns everything in the mountains. There's been a long dry spell. Men like the Honeywells, practically everyone under the mountains, haven't done very well lately. In fact, they're about done."

That was an old story. Clay and his father had been close to range trouble before; and they had always ridden clear without involvement.

"The hill ranchers tried to force their way onto Lone Star range, and they couldn't make it stick," Bitsy said. "That's the size of it."

"Yeah," Dutch said. "That's all. It's plenty."

It wasn't much, Clay thought, just other men's troubles. He wondered now why he had even bothered to ask about the situation.

Habit urged Clay one way; rebellion made him say to Bitsy, "Drink?"

"Do you want one?"

"Yes."

14

Bitsy started toward a table. "Two of your best, Dutch."

After he was seated it occurred to Clay that he had seen men pull out chairs for women. Bitsy gave no indication that she was aware of his lack of courtesy.

She studied him across the table. "You certainly put a scare into the Honeywells."

"Not one bit, but the others scared themselves." Clay watched an amused expression spread on Bitsy's face. Her jaw line was strong and clean. There was no coarseness about her features at all.

Footsteps that hurried unevenly were coming from the back part of the saloon. Billy Smithers, Clay thought; the man's feet had sounded like that when he came twisting through the front door to warn the hill ranchers. There was his reward, partly consumed, on the bar.

Smithers was headed toward the bottle when he saw Clay and Bitsy. He skidded in the sand as he stopped. For a moment the bottle pulled him one way and a fear that leaped across his face at the sight of Clay held him where he was. He came to the table slowly, using both hands to help him talk.

"I wasn't in that thing at all, mister. I just happened to be near the livery stable when the Honeywells rode in. They said for me— You understand I wasn't in it at all—They said for me— I like Jim Krimble; but they said—"

Smithers began to back up. "I got no pistol, mister. I ain't no fighting man! They said . . ." Still talking, he backed to the bar, caught the bottle by the neck and trotted from the room like a small animal headed for its burrow.

Bitsy's gaze had never turned from Clay's face.

"Why did he think you were going to shoot him?"

The tone was like one of those learning questions Jeff was fond of asking, not to find out something but to explain something. Clay shook his head. "He knew better."

"No, he didn't," Bitsy said. "You look at all men with the same cold expression. What causes it?"

"I don't know. I just look."

"It's what you're thinking that makes you so grim and cold. You look at me that way, almost."

Dutch came bumping over with two drinks. Clay gave Bitsy a sharp look. The drinks were lemonade.

Bitsy smiled. "Dutch says you pour whiskey in the gabboon, cowboy." She sipped her drink. "What's your name?"

"Clay Arbuckle." The sheriff had known. Clay tried to make out if the name meant anything to Bitsy. She read his intention and shook her head.

"Clay for Clayton?" she asked.

He nodded.

"It seems to me I've heard that name," Dutch said.

Clay looked at him over the rim of his glass. "There's no reason you should have."

"Well, I thought . . ." Dutch went back to the bar.

Jim Krimble walked into the Horseshoe as if he owned it. He merely glanced at Clay. Every feature of Krimble's face was bluntly cast. The flesh of middle age was riding his shoulders. His brows were black and straight, his eyes the color of water in a deep cave.

Chauncey Wade was a step behind Krimble. Wade's Roman nose and cold blue eyes were set in Clay's direction all the time the man was following Krimble to the bar.

Two right-siders, Clay thought. One was arrogant and

16

sure; the other icy and sure. No wonder the hill men had thought six too few.

Krimble put his back to the bar. His glance took in the lemonade glasses, and passed briefly over Clay's face. Chauncey Wade kept staring thoughtfully at Clay.

"How are you, Bitsy?" Krimble asked.

"Fine, Jim. How's Alice?"

"Good, good. She'll be in next week. She thought maybe you'd help her with a dress fitting at Mrs. Archer's."

"I'll be glad to."

Krimble turned back to the bar. Dutch had set out a bottle and two glasses. "That's what you wanted, wasn't it, Jim?"

"As long as it's wet." Krimble poured a drink for Wade and then one for himself. "What happened, Dutch?"

"Well— Ask him." Dutch looked over at Clay.

"I asked you." Krimble did not turn.

"The Honeywells came riding in, up the street. The others slipped over the hill and left their horses out of sight. They came from the north, that is. I guess—"

"Ben told me that part. I mean in here."

Dutch looked at Clay. Wade also turned his hawk-nosed face, but Krimble's heavy neck and shoulders did not move. "Go on, Dutch. What happened? You were here."

"They lost their sand, everybody but Anse and Barr."

"Why?" Krimble asked.

"Arbuckle there sort of chilled 'em."

Krimble drank his whiskey. "How?"

Dutch spoke in the tone of one who thought his answer weak. "Just sitting there. That was all there was to it, Jim."

17

Krimble nodded. "Andrews pulled away first?"

Dutch nodded.

"Then Callaway?"

"No, Limberis."

"Uh-huh," Krimble said, as if the whole matter was of no importance. "Thanks, Dutch. Another one, Chaunce?"

Wade shook his head. He wiped the back of his hand across his clipped mustache and the gesture turned his head toward Clay for an instant.

"I guess we got the story," Krimble said. He and Wade went out.

Bitsy had been watching Clay. "What did you think of Krimble?"

Clay answered absently. "Both on the right."

"That's an odd way to say it, but I'm glad you see their side."

"I mean—" For a moment Clay considered an explanation, and then he realized it would take more talking than he had done at one stretch since he was a kid; and then maybe Bitsy wouldn't understand.

"If you're looking for a job, Mr. Arbuckle, you could ask Jim Krimble," Bitsy said.

"He never hires any—" Dutch stopped. He was back in his own mental stew once more.

"Never hires any what?" Bitsy asked.

"Very many riders at this time of year. You know that, Bitsy." Dutch blinked at his feeble cover-up. "What I meant to say—"

Bitsy interrupted again before he hung himself beyond recovery. "You started to say he never hires any pistol fighters or toughs. What makes you think Mr. Arbuckle is one?"

"Oh, I don't!" Some native honesty in Dutch made

18

him scowl at himself. He gave up and began to polish the bar.

Painfully short of conversational material, Clay merely sat and looked at Bitsy. Never before had he considered inability to talk a handicap.

She asked, "Do you always keep your chair out from the table like that?"

Clay nodded. Bitsy's teeth were clean and white. There was no cornstarch dust or paint on her face. He guessed she didn't need either. He began to wonder if old Jeff knew all there was to know about women.

"You never fiddle with your glass—or make any nervous motions with your hands, do you?" Bitsy asked.

"I guess not," he said. He felt like a big lump sitting there contributing nothing to the talk. He cupped his fingers over the top of his empty glass, turning it slowly against the scarred table. Then all at once the gesture struck him as childish and he felt awkward and uneasy. Bitsy watched him curiously.

He rose quickly from the table. "I got to eat now." He wondered why he bothered to explain when all he had to do was leave.

"Come back again," Bitsy said.

"Yeah, drop in anytime," Dutch called, but it was evident that Clay's leaving made the saloon man feel better. Clay crossed the street and started on toward the hotel, where he and Jeff had checked in late the night before. Wavell was still at his desk, not singing now, but sitting there tapping the toes of his soft shoes with the broom.

"Come in, Arbuckle. I was just going to eat, and I never like to eat alone. Half the world's trouble comes from eating alone. Bad for digestion too." Wavell tossed the broom toward a corner. When he rose the shift from

19

the awkward position at the desk was done with spring steel ease. "Jim and old Chaunce looked you over, huh?"

Clay nodded.

"And that was all?"

"That was all."

The sheriff went toward a door at the back of the office. "Come in and wash up. I think maybe I even got a curry comb that'll go through that hair of yours." He ran his hand over his own thin sandy hair. "I was a good looking lad once myself, in an ugly sort of way, that is."

The sheriff's living quarters were comfortably dusty and untidy. Wavell motioned toward a washstand. "Go ahead. I've got a clean towel around somewhere, I think."

While Clay washed, Wavell poked around the room until he found a stack of towels on a curtained shelf, with several boxes of cartridges and a broken rifle stock. He tossed a towel to Clay, looked reflectively at the broken stock, and then returned it to the shelf.

"Right handed, Arbuckle?"

Clay's pistol was on the left side but he had caught the towel with his right hand, and now he remembered that he had picked up the broom with his right hand also.

"Either hand," he said.

They walked toward the hotel. The air was still and the odor of old dust seemed to be hanging in it.

"How long, O Lord, how long?" Wavell said. "I can't remember when it rained last." He looked toward the hills. "It'll take more than rain now." A heavy mood settled on him and he did not speak again until they were near the hotel.

"I'll stake you to an introduction to a pretty girl,

20

Arbuckle. Vanita Krimble, Jim's girl. She ought to be eating about now."

Clay expected to see the blue blouse and the riding skirt but the girl alone at a table was starch and white lace. She was the same one he had seen earlier. She did not look anything at all like Jim Krimble.

Wavell dumped his hat on a rack. "Come on, come on," he said when Clay hesitated. "Vanita won't eat you, not for a minute or two at least."

The girl smiled. "Why not, Ben?" Her eyes were smoky gray.

The sheriff introduced Clay, who thought a moment, nodded and then said, "How'd do, Miss Krimble."

"You can invite us to set and eat, Nita," Wavell said. "You can even pay for my grub if you want to."

"I'll take you up on that someday, and then watch you start backing out," Vanita said. "Sit down, Mr. Arbuckle. There's no need to invite Ben, as you can see."

A woman came for the orders. "Steak or stew."

Wavell groaned. "I ought to get married and escape this. How about it, Nita, can you cook?"

"I make awful good taffy, Ben." Vanita was looking at Clay, probing at him, balancing what she saw against something she was thinking. "You're the one that ran the coyotes away from my father's back, Mr. Arbuckle. Why?"

"Arbuckle was an innocent bystander," Wavell said. "He set in Dutch's place, and a bunch of cowards scared themselves plumb out of town."

"The Honyewells are not cowards, Ben." Vanita kept watching Clay thoughtfully.

"Steak or stew?" the waitress asked.

"Steak, about half done as usual," Wavell said.

21

Clay nodded at the waitress and she left.

"No, Anse and Barr are not cowards," Wavell said. "But maybe they felt a little guilty in advance, going at things the way they did. Guilt is some the same as being afraid."

"Sheriff Ben Wavell, philosopher," Vanita said, still studying Clay. "You might be right, Ben. A really strong man probably never admits guilt when it might interfere with what he has to do."

"Speaking of your father, where is he?" Wavell asked.

"Seeing a lawyer about more land titles. What I said was right, wasn't it, Mr. Arbuckle?"

"I don't know," Clay said.

Vanita laughed. "I'll bet you don't! You must have quite a reputation, a following too no doubt."

"No posses on his tail," Wavell said.

"Sometimes you're not a bit funny, Ben." Vanita's voice was cold. Clay sensed that she really did not like Wavell, in spite of her easy banter with him. "You do have a reputation as a pistolman, don't you, Mr. Arbuckle?"

That was something for Clay to consider now. As far as he knew Wavell was the only man who had ever recognized him offhand. "Get a reputation and get killed," Jeff always said.

The time Clay had been forced to shoot two gamblers in New Mexico Jeff had given the marshal false names for himself and Clay. Now Clay was wondering; it was not his name that marked him wherever he went. It was something else he carried, and even women noticed. Jeff said women were merely tricky and always after something, but they were probably just as smart as men, Clay decided.

22

Vanita dropped her probing suddenly. Her smile was just as friendly as Bitsy's. "I didn't mean to pry into your private life, Mr. Arbuckle."

"On behalf of Mr. Arbuckle, I accept your apologies for poking into his business," Wavell said. "When's the next dance somewhere, Nita? I got to get some politicking done."

"You'd better do it with a jug out by the buggies," the girl said. "That dancing of yours won't win any votes."

Wavell and Vanita laughed. How could they do that? Clay wondered. They didn't like each other, he was sure, but still they could carry on lightly. He went through the meal uneasily while the other two talked. They did not leave him out; they explained events and names that he did not understand, and that made him realize all the more that he was an outsider.

Tonight or tomorrow—he and Jeff might ride on. But why couldn't they settle sometime where people were friendly, where faces meant companionship and talk, instead of impressions to be stored against some future possibility of violence.

Why couldn't he and Jeff stay here?

From the window of his room Clay watched Vanita go across the street to her father and Wade in front of a lawyer's office. Wavell went toward the Horseshoe, his hat on the back of his head, his shoes slapping little clouds of dust. He wore no pistol; an odd sheriff.

The walls of the room creaked with heat. Far across the scorched hills there were snow streaks on the mountains. Cool winds and green trees edging high meadows up there, and water running over ancient gravel . . . The hills this side were gray. They were the gray life Clay had been riding through, the dust of yesterday, and they were, also, the dust of tomorrow.

23

Why shouldn't gaunt men like the Honeywells reach toward the mountains? And why shouldn't Krimble stand tough and spraddle-legged on what was his? It was other folks' business, simple, clear cut. Stay away from it.

Jeff had made the lesson stick when Clay was about fifteen. In a Kansas trail town they saw three toughs beating a Texas rider with fists and pistols. One of the cowboy's arms was broken. His scalp was hanging over one ear and his mouth was a bloody hole.

Without trying to think, Clay put his pistol on the three toughs. Two backed down; the third one spun the pistol in his hand and so Clay shot him in the arm. The cowboy said, "Thanks, shaver," and collapsed like a soft rag.

Clay moved to help him and then Jeff hooked his arm around his son's neck and jerked him back. "That wasn't one bit your show." Jeff's eyes were sparking mad. He spun Clay around and knocked the pistol from his hand.

"But there were three—"

Jeff knocked Clay cold with one punch.

Sometime later Clay came out of it, lying on the floor of a livery stable where Jeff had carried him. Jeff helped him up and brushed some of the filth from his son's clothes. "Two things bad wrong about that," Jeff said. "It was none of your call, to start. The second one, you got fancy with your shooting. The target on a man is somewhere in a straight line between his chin and belt buckle—or else you don't shoot at all. You understand?"

Clay couldn't forget the cowboy's face. "But—"

Jeff knocked him cold again. It was the last time he ever touched his son in anger, and thereafter Clay never tried to help another man.

And yet he could not forget the memory of the beaten cowboy who had said, "Thanks, shaver." No one afterward ever said thanks to Clay for anything. He always figured that he owed that Texas man more than the man owed him.

And still haunting him was the memory of lightning splitting a rainy night, of bellowing cattle with fire on their horn tips. That must have been very long ago, for he had no memories of anything before that night.

There had been, later, a tall bearded man who seldom laughed, and a huge fair-haired woman who wore half boots and worked beside her husband in a wheat field. Ed and Bertha. They lived in a great flat valley somewhere in the past.

How long he lived in the wheat valley Clay did not know. Late one afternoon a rider towing a saddled horse came to the house. The sky was muttering. The heat was sticky. Ed and Bertha were far away in a field. They started running toward the house when they saw the rider.

The man's face was bitter-quiet about a curling black beard. There was a deadness in his eyes.

"What's your name, boy?"

Stranger-cautious, Clay stood just outside the doorway, twisting his bare feet. He did not answer.

"Come over here."

Clay shook his head.

"Christ's sake, boy! Don't you wear shoes?"

Ed and Bertha never minded if he went barefoot.

"Not your business," he told the man. Ed and Bertha didn't like cowboys anyway.

The man swung down, walking with a limp back to the second horse. "Can you ride, Clay?"

25

Clay was startled; the man knew his name.

Sometimes Clay rode in from the field on one of the broad workhorses. He liked horses and he could drive them too and help harness them, but that also was none of this man's business. Clay did not like him.

The fellow made a small approving nod. "An empty barrel is noisy. Remember that, Clay."

Bertha's face was red when she reached the yard, but when she saw the rider her color changed until there were only red spots left against a grayness. Ed fingered his beard. Neither of them said hello to the stranger. It was he who told Clay to stay outside when the three of them went into the house.

Clay walked over to the watering trough, glad to be relieved of talking to the black-bearded man. He heard little of what was said inside, except when Bertha spoke.

"But you wait!" she said. "Tonight is rain." She said other sentences in a protesting tone but the stranger's low voice always cut across her own and stopped it.

They came outside. Bertha's face was wooden. Ed kept stroking his beard helplessly. His eyes were sad when he looked at Clay.

"This man is your father," Bertha said. "Now you will go with him."

The last Clay saw of Bertha she was standing by the rain barrel in her rough shoes and ragged dress. The muscles of her face seemed to have sagged all in lumps down around her wide mouth. All of a sudden she turned away, Ed put his arms around her, patting her back.

Fourteen years later, here in the hotel in South Fork, Clay wondered if he had learned anything since that afternoon. The skills he knew, he discounted. What he did not know loomed very large, for it included almost the entire field of human relationship.

His shifting life, never more than three months in one place, coupled with a natural shyness of others, which Jeff had built into distrust, had left Clay with no normal linkage to other human beings. All that ever reached out from the isolation bounded by his skin was a shrewd and deadly appraisal of fellow men.

This he had recognized some time before, and the need of changing it had grown in him until it was an explosive force. He sensed he was at the point where he would turn either toward hating all men forever or toward being one of them.

Maybe he had started one way or the other today.

He got off the bed and went to the washstand near the window. The face in the mirror was just the same as it had been when he looked at himself between the fluted columns in the Horseshoe.

Clay saw nothing to mark him as a pistol fighter who had killed five men, for he was looking out, not in.

Staring at the set composure of his face, he tried a smile. It was forced, moving muscles that felt stiff. He looked, he decided, like a snarling dog. No, he was not cut out for smiling, not even when something faintly touched a feeling of amusement in him.

As if to hurl it out the window, he snatched the white pitcher from the washstand, and then he stood looking at the hand he had tried to use unconsciously. It was the right hand.

From his warbag on a chair he took a holster almost like the one on the bed, except that it was for the right side. Jeff would notice the change instantly. Maybe Jeff noticed too many things too quick.

Clay had just completed changing scabbards and was

holding the gun belt when the knock sounded. There was no friend to come through the door, he knew. Habits instilled in him long ago took control and moved him against the wall before he said, "Come."

It was Vanita Krimble. Quite coolly she looked at the pistol close to Clay's right hand, and then she smiled. "I didn't mean to spook you." She closed the door behind her.

"My father is stubborn, Mr. Arbuckle. He's also very tough, but today you saw only a few of the men who are against him. He needs help. I want you to help him."

"He didn't come."

"He won't either. I came. You can get a job at Window Sash. That's about five miles east of the Lone Star home place. Billy Nairn owns the Sash. See him."

"Riding work?"

Her eyes were harder to read than a man's. "Of course. Will you take it?"

Clay rolled the idea over a few times, trying to weigh it against Vanita's purpose. If she were a man, he would know better where to place her.

"Well?" She was not impatient, but there was a solid demanding quality behind the word.

Clay said, "I'll see."

"See before tomorrow night. If the man who came here with you wants a job, take him too."

She was turning toward the door when a point of frayed lace on her dress front caught her eyes. She tried to press the lace in place with her fingers; and she was still frowning down at it when she went out and left the door open.

A little later he saw her walk across the street, going toward the lawyer's office. Even out there in the hot hands of the sun, she still appeared cool. Her dress did not restrain her walk to a mince, but the movement of her body was entirely female.

Clay stared at the open doorway after she disappeared.

He stood for a moment and then went slowly downstairs; by the time he crossed the lobby his face was in its habitual grave set. The clerk, ready to shift his eyes if the man looked at him suddenly, saw the same fellow who had gone upstairs not long before.

The clerk licked his lips, and went back to the kitchen to give his views to the cook concerning pistol fighters.

Outside, Clay stood under the wooden awning. It was scarcely cooler in the shade than in the sun, a fact which he did not consider at all. Jeff had taught him that there were no physical discomforts in the world, merely men who whined about cold or heat or wetness.

The sheriff came from Dutch's place with Krimble and Wade. The two men started across the street with Wavell, and then they saw Clay. They turned and went back to the other side and on to the lawyer's office. Wavell sauntered over to his own office.

Lesser men would not have changed their minds, Clay knew; lesser men who wore pistols would have come right on past him, proving something to themselves, trying to prove something to him.

As he went down the street he watched a dust cloud boiling off the first hill west. Two riders coming into town. Wavell called out when Clay started to pass the sheriff's office.

"Come in, Arbuckle. It's hotter in here than outside." The sheriff was changing his sox at his desk. He blew sand from his shoes, slipped them on and leaned back in his chair.

He did not give a hang who saw those shoes, Clay

29

thought. Wavell was just plain natural, and maybe that was why Clay thought he liked the man. Clay put his foot on a chair; he was not yet to the point of sitting down.

Wavell began to roll a cigarette. "Did somebody make you an offer, Arbuckle?"

"Offer of what?"

"Work."

Clay fell back on habit, searching the sheriff's face for motive, looking for all the little signs which betray a man's thoughts.

Wavell was undisturbed by Clay's silence. "Krimble would never admit that Lone Star can't take care of itself. His daughter would."

"I don't hire out to fight."

"That's what I thought," Wavell said. The full force of his eyes struck Clay. They were shrewdly questioning eyes now, but friendly. He licked his cigarette and put it to his mouth.

Billy Smithers skidded into the office, panting, filling the place with whiskey odor. "They're coming—the Honeywells again!"

Wavell tried his coat pockets for matches. He found one and lit his cigarette. "Let them come, Billy."

"Well, ain't you going to—"

"No, I ain't." Wavell kept looking at Smithers, and finally the little man backed out of the office. "Well, I thought you ought to know," he said in an injured tone.

Wavell put his feet on the desk. It was not a pose at all, Clay decided. The man was utterly relaxed in body, but his mind was working sharply. There was nothing to be gained by motion, nothing to be found out until the Honeywells arrived.

They had pushed their horses hard, but not too hard,

30

Clay saw, when the brothers swung down at the hitchrack in front of the office. Barr waited for Anse. They saw Clay at the same time, and an instant later, as if by agreement, they both were consciously ignoring him.

"Somebody got Sam Andrews from the rocks this side of Little Squaw crossing an hour ago." Anse Honeywell spoke evenly, with accusation coloring his tone.

Wavell did not move. "Tell me, Anse."

"Barr and me were about a quarter mile ahead of the others. We heard the shot and saw 'em scatter, and we went back. Sam was dead when he went out of the saddle."

Andrews had been the little one with the gray mustache, Clay remembered. Fear had driven him from one place and death had caught him at another; and that was all the reaction there was in Clay Arbuckle.

"Rifle?" Wavell asked.

"One shot," Anse said.

"You went up on the ridge?"

Anse nodded. "A while afterward, yes. Barr and me, came in at the ends of it. There wasn't any sign at all."

Clay saw men gathering in doorways across the street. All morning they had stayed inside. A fat man in a butcher's apron waddled over and stood outside on the walk. Billy Smithers' purple-veined nose showed around the jamb, and then he edged inside, staring from the sheriff to the Honeywells with mouth half open.

"You were a quarter of a mile ahead, huh, Anse?" Wavell asked.

Some men might have taken offense, or given a sharp answer. "About," Anse said.

Barr Honeywell moved his head slowly to look at

31

Clay. He was the older of the two, Clay decided; it showed in the neck muscles. There were other small differences, but both the brothers belonged on the right side of the bush, close together. Dust on Barr's long face brought out the whites of his eyes as he gave Clay a steady look from the wells under deep brow arches.

"You've got it straight now," Anse said to Wavell. "You know who started things."

"Uh-huh. They were all together, huh—Sam, Olin Limberis, Callaway, and Tol Shepherd?"

Anse nodded. "All together, on neutral ground."

"Like the Horseshoe this morning, huh?"

Anse flattened his lips. "Nothing happened this morning, Ben. It's happened now."

"And I'm the sheriff."

"That's it."

Wavell stood up. "My tail is not in a crack, Anse. I'll do what there is to do." His powerful hands and the sudden toughness of his gaze did not fit with his rosy cheeks and mild jaw as he leaned on his desk and said, "You boys didn't much try to stop it when it could have been stopped, did you?"

Anse said, "Did Krimble?"

"No. Nobody did, including me."

"The others took Sam on up to his place," Anse said, "in case you're wanting to have a look at him."

"They just dumped him across his horse, huh, figuring to ride up to the door and call his wife out?"

"I told Limberis to go on ahead."

Wavell nodded. "That poor damned woman. She didn't have things bad enough before . . ."

Anse looked once at Clay, and then the brothers went outside. Smithers jumped sidewise to clear the way. Several men had joined the butcher now. "What

32

happened, Anse?"

The Honeywells went up on their horses. "Somebody killed Sam Andrews. Come on, Barr."

Sam Andrews . . . Maybe he was just a little more than a face seen briefly in the Horseshoe, Clay thought. There had been six of them, and for a few moments he had wanted to slide along the bar and stand with them and be noticed only as another man. Sam Andrews probably had harmed no one in all his life.

A few hours before, following the rigid channel of his own interest, Clay had felt nothing but contempt for Andrews because he was so far to the left of the bush that he was only a blur seen from the corner of the eye.

But for the dead there was no contempt. What then did he feel concerning Andrews? Clay was not sure. He fell back on habit: it was none of his affair.

"You figure on a posse, Ben?" Smithers asked eagerly. "I'll go tell everybody. I'll—"

"Are you a good tracker, Arbuckle?"

Clay said, "Fair." He could follow a coyote through sage brush. There had been months when that was about all he had to do. Jeff had taught him plenty about the marks of animals and men.

"Do you want to ride along with me?" Wavell asked.

Clay shook his head.

"That's what I figured," Wavell said cheerfully. "Smithers, you want to scamper, so how about beating me to Frost's barn and telling Hard to saddle up Jingo?"

Smithers ducked out and trotted up the street.

Wavell stood a moment, chewing his lower lip, looking at the rifle rack. "This might bust things, all right. Close the door when you leave, will you, Arbuckle?"

Out on the walk, Wavell shook his head at the quick

33

questions. "Just what Anse told you. That's all I know right now."

The group of merchants and townspeople watched Wavell walk away in his Congress gaiters. Worry was probing at them. Someone cursed Krimble, and someone defended him and cursed the Honeywells.

"They gabble their heads off in towns," Jeff always said. "They deefen a man with nothing."

Clay saw Dutch and Bitsy standing in front of the Horseshoe. The fat butcher, who had been closer than anyone else to the door while Anse Honeywell was talking, tried to tell what he had heard. Someone who had heard a little more, or something different, began an argument with the butcher over details.

"Ask *him,* damn you!" The butcher pointed at Clay.

Gravely watching the expressions of the people outside, Clay knew no one would ask him about the conversation. He told himself he did not care; but when, after studying him doubtfully, the townsmen went away, he wondered how difficult it would have been to have stepped out and told them what they wanted to know.

He stood where he was until Wavell rode past. *I could have gone with him*, Clay thought. *Was there any good reason why I could not?* He went out, closing the door carefully.

Gathered before their places of business, the merchants of the town talked in low voices, looking now and then toward Clay.

Bitsy called, "Mr. Arbuckle!" Her voice put a quietness on the street.

Clay started toward her, not hurrying. Wavell was just going out of town, moving briskly but not trying to kill his horse. Men began to edge toward the Horseshoe.

With one eye on approaching business, Dutch took

34

the bar towel from his shoulder and shook it out. He kicked a pebble from the walk. "Who got Andrews?" he asked.

"Nobody knows."

"Family man." Dutch snapped his towel again. "That won't help things none at all. How did Anse take it?"

"Quiet," Clay said. Dutch was losing his awe of Clay, and Clay liked him better for it.

Bitsy shook her head. "The Honeywells didn't have any idea about it?"

Clay told her briefly what Anse had reported. Dutch repeated the answers loudly, in the guise of questions. The butcher was the first to approach, and then others came. Bitsy and Clay had to move away from the doorway. Dutch led his customers inside, tolling them along with a repetition of what Clay had said.

Bitsy looked down at her dress. "I'd better change and go out to the Andrews place." All at once there was doubt of Clay that he had not seen before. "You didn't come here to—"

"No."

"Honestly?"

"I'd never heard of South Fork when my father said we'd try here."

"Try what?"

Sometimes that expression of Jeff's had bothered Clay, also. "Try for work, what else?" Jeff always answered; and now Clay gave Bitsy the same answer.

She seemed to forget her doubt at once. "I've got to ride out there."

Dancehall girls did not generally ride anywhere. They did not know ranchers' wives on personal terms, either. It was none of Clay's business.

Bitsy took the question from his face. "My father was

35

a small rancher here several years ago. He was the first one to starve out. He had good luck doing that wherever he happened to be. Montana was the place, he said. Before that, it had been a half dozen other places—as long as I could remember.

"My mother went with him. I didn't. Dutch is my uncle, my mother's brother. He stays in one place." Bitsy went back into the Horseshoe. Clay saw her walk the length of the big room and disappear into a hall at the back.

One of the drinkers at the bar was saying, "I seen the four of them when they eased into town. I couldn't figure out just what was up, until I seen the Honeywells ride in a little later. Sam was never one for fighting, but I guess when a man's cattle are starving . . ."

No one spoke to Clay as he walked up the street. Bitsy was going out of town. Ben Wavell was already gone. There was the hotel room. There was the Horseshoe. Waiting. He had waited for Jeff countless times before in forgotten towns. There must be better things to do.

He could have gone with the sheriff.

Hound-dog lonesome . . . studying men in bunkhouses, in crowded saloons. Never one of them, merely weighing them and watching them for treachery.

He passed the livery stable where his gelding was. Stablemen generally liked to talk and gossip. Almost any man could pass an idle half hour in a stable. Last night the barn man had started chattering almost before he was awake.

And then when his lantern light fell full on Clay and Jeff, he had stopped his gabble in the middle of a sentence.

Clay walked out of town to a dry creek bed littered

with crates and other debris. The distance clearly brought out South Fork's position on dreary flatness. There were wells behind the buildings. Not much farther west the hills would have given some wind protection and perhaps running water the year around.

Some towns were like some men. There wasn't much excuse for their being where they were or the way they were.

Gravel skittered down the edge of the bank across from Clay, and then he saw a rattlesnake twisting toward a hole. He threw dirt on it with his first bullet to drive it into striking position. His next shot mangled the flattish head.

He knew that the accuracy of his second shot, over the distance it had carried, would have brought a startled look from any man who knew how difficult a pistol was to handle well. Once there had been pleasure in the knowledge that he was a master pistol shot.

One time at a ranch where he and Jeff worked for a short period, Clay had driven shingle nails into a board at fifteen paces, sheerly for the pleasure of seeing admiration on the faces of the other cowboys.

Coldly furious, Jeff had drawled, "What are you—a stinking show-off?"

He looked back at the town. Tiny figures were running into the street, trying to see why he had shot. For a moment he was of a mind to empty his pistol into the writhing rope across the creek bed; but he reloaded, and stood there looking at the green slopes that Jim Krimble was holding against other men.

Billy Nairn—that was the name of the man Vanita Krimble said to see. Clay wondered why he had let her go away carrying the idea that he might go out to Nairn's Window Sash.

37

He went back to South Fork, moving with careful strides. His outer face was a sterile field, solemn but not calm.

Three men were standing in the doorway of Frost's livery stable. They were silent as Clay passed. Afterward, one said, "Practicing. They have to all the time, them kind of hard cookies. Who sent for him?"

Not long after the sun went down the town was full of men. There were horses at every hitchrack and more animals than tie space at the rail in front of the Horseshoe.

Like the men who had ridden them, the horses showed a belly-tightened look from fighting years of drought. Men went in and out of Dutch's place aimlessly, it seemed; but they lacked the loudness that often goes with loafing.

They drank coffee in the Comet Cafe, close to the dark office of the sheriff. They leaned against the building, talking of Sam Andrews. South Fork was so far from everywhere, Clay thought, that it must never have been a tough town. One killing had caused a buzzing mutter, underlaid with dread.

The whole area apparently was disturbed. Clay tried to understand why one simple killing could lay such a cold hand on so many people. He judged the conversations that he overheard. There was no talk of vengeance, merely speculation and fear.

Reassurance, he guessed, was what they wanted. They grouped up to find it, asking each other what should be done, probably deciding as individuals to do nothing at all.

Clay fought with a badly cooked steak in the Comet Cafe, his presence putting strain on the conversation of other customers. He knew now: they recognized him for what he was, and they were suspicious of his position in the trouble. For reasons of his own, obscure even to himself, he had sided against the Honeywells. Krimble had not even said thanks for the act.

No wonder no one knew where Clay stood.

Someone at the counter said, "This'll put us all in a hole. We all got to live in the country."

Clay was moved to contempt for the man and everyone like him; and then it came to him that the trouble belonged to everyone in the South Fork country. The residents could not, like Clay, merely move on to avoid an unpleasant situation.

What made settled people different from Clay and Jeff? Clay never before had bothered to consider the question, for Jeff always said that settled people were ham-strung people. Maybe they were not that way at all; maybe they figured they owed something to their neighbors and the country they lived in.

They could not make all decisions on a personal basis, the simple way. They had to gabble and worry, but perhaps they tried to do what was best for all. All of Jeff's decisions were for himself and Clay, and Clay had never found anything wrong about that, except . . . the simple way was also the lonely way.

Clay was beginning to feel terror because of the loneliness that stalked inside him.

He did not eat all of his meal.

As he went up the street he saw men standing by the hitchracks, sitting on benches in front of buildings, sober men together in the sticky dusk. His passing left a ripple of silence.

Long after midnight he was still awake on his bed, listening to the heat creaking from the timbers of the

39

hotel. Like a cross current in the coolness just beginning to wash down from the mountains, the murmur and stirring of men still came from the street.

He heard his father on the stairs. The uneven tread, light on one foot, settling heavily on the other, came to the door. Jeff rattled the knob; it was his way of knocking. When the door gave way unexpectedly, Clay heard his father leap aside.

"Here," Clay said.

Jeff locked the door behind him. Boards sawed against each other in the floor as he went to the window. The roller shade came down all the way and then tore from its fastenings. The coil spring whirred angrily in the darkness, and the odor of ancient dust drifted over to Clay.

Jeff unlashed his bedroll and hung a blanket over the window. "A locked door gives a man a little time," he said.

Time for what? Clay's whole life had been ordered by flat statements like that.

The lamp showed the gray in Jeff's beard. During the last few years the flesh had tightened against his heavy cheekbones.

"Where was I born?" Clay asked.

Jeff took off his shirt and coat and dropped them on his bedroll. He went to the mirror, moving his head from side to side as he studied his face.

"Where was I born, Jeff?"

"A little place in Kentucky."

"No longhorns there."

Jeff's face was puddled with shadows when he turned. The wary stillness of an animal was on him instantly. "Still that stampede, huh?"

"That much I remember."

"You were three when we moved from Kentucky."

"What was a three-year-old doing on a trail drive?"

"You were older than three when that happened." Jeff poured water in the basin. He began to strop Clay's razor.

"What happened to Marta, my mother?"

Quick ferocity spun Jeff from his task. The gray steel of the razor glinted as he pointed at Clay. "I said not to mention her name."

Clay sat up. He tugged his boots off, and then he sat on the edge of the bed, staring across his shoulder at his father. The blanket over the window had made the room sifling hot again.

Jeff began to lather his face. There was hot water in the kitchen, for the asking, but cold was good enough for Jeff. Ever since the gray had started in his beard he had been threatening to shave clean.

Clay said, "I'm tired of batting around like this."

Jeff worked the lather in. The cold scrape of the razor sounded high on one cheek. He stood with his hat tipped back, making short slanting strokes, stropping the razor at frequent intervals.

"I'm staying here," Clay said.

Jeff might not have heard. He shaved as he did everything, bluntly and without regard for comfort. He wiped the accumulations of lather and hair on an old newspaper. There was not a speck of blood on his face when he had finished his work.

The pale new face made Clay stare. There was a maze of tiny lines the beard had covered, and the top furrows of the spoke-like wrinkles at the corners of Jeff's eyes were now clearly defined almost to the tips of small flat ears; and the bitter, seeking expression of the eyes was more dominant than before.

41

"You made a good start at staying," Jeff said. "You and your sheriff chum sandwiching the Honeywell boys like that."

Clay was not surprised; Jeff had a way of finding out what had happened during his absences.

"I made no play at all," Clay said.

"You didn't walk out of the Horseshoe when you should have. What's this about staying here? I didn't say we would."

"I'm staying. I got a job."

"Where?"

"Window Sash."

Jeff removed his gunbelt and hung it on the bed post. Without comment he observed that Clay had shifted holsters. "A dirty gun, an unlocked door," Jeff said, after he had lifted Clay's pistol. "This town and the women you've been hanging around have made you careless."

"You can have a job at the Sash," Clay said.

"Suppose I say we're moving on?"

Clay shook his head.

His pistol struck the bed near his right hand. Jeff's face was screwed down to a steadiness that was almost blankness. "We're riding on tonight, Clay."

Long ago Clay had put his father on the right, and that was all that ran through Clay's mind now. His father's hand would come sweeping up to the butt grips of the pistol hanging on the bed post; but the holster would swing, binding the pistol just a little. Clay merely had to reach and fire, with his elbow resting on the bed. In a split second it was laid out that way in his mind.

Affecting the simplicity was one concession: he would shoot Jeff in the shoulder.

"I'm staying, Jeff."

42

Jeff waited a moment longer. The faint smile came. He nodded slowly. "You've been taught good." And then there was a quick afterthought. "Just where were you going to shoot?"

"Shoulder."

"You poor damn fool!" Somewhere in the ruthless depths of Jeff's character a flame spouted high and threw a savage light across his face. "Have I wasted my time on an idiot?"

With his muscles suddenly flat, Clay stared at the floor. He was just like his father; he knew only one way to settle an issue. There were no human qualities in either of them, no give, no warmth. Clay thought of Wavell's mud face and easy chatter; he wished that he had gone with the sheriff.

Jeff tried the lock. He tilted the back of a chair under the doorknob, and began to undress. "I had us both jobs at Seven Cross, but go ahead and take the one at Sash. It won't hurt to sort of split up for a while."

"There's trouble here."

"I heard," Jeff said. "We can't dodge it forever." He seemed quite cheerful.

They rode out of South Fork before sun-up. In the early light the town was as bleak as fog, gray boards and dead windows. To the west the hills lay in sullen heaps, as if they, like the little ranchers, resented the greenness of the mountains.

Jeff was grim. He never met a morning as anything but the start of another day. He held his sorrel in with a hard rein when it would have broken into a warming run. To Jeff, a horse was a tool to be used and cared for, and that was the end of the relationship.

Clay had been taught to regard any animal the same way.

They followed a road that twisted in the small valleys between the hills. Here and there was a trace of moisture in the bottom, but the hills were scorched. The feet of the horses made soft plops and the dust came up gray in the still air.

"Dry," Clay said.

His father gave him a brief, contemptuous look.

They came to a small stream, green edged. It grew as they went higher in the hills. Shortly before the road veered right across the stream to slant sharply up a rocky hogback, Clay stopped his red roan. Horseshoes and boots had left many marks here. He saw the wide, flat imprints of shoes that must have belonged to Ben Wavell.

On the left, the jumble of a steep rock escarpment came at the river in a sharp angle. That would be Little Squaw crossing there ahead, and here was where Sam Andrews had been shot.

Clay stared up at the ridge. Pale rocks with the sun just touching on them. It must have been an easy shot. Andrews had been a scared little man. Why him? Why not one of the Honeywells? It was just a ridge, and this was just a trampled place beside a road, but someone, Andrews' wife, could never ride past here or hear the name Little Squaw crossing without feeling the bite of black remembrance.

It was not sympathy with Clay; he did not know Andrews' widow and he did not know the feel of sympathy to be recognized as such. He guessed he was wondering a little about the thoughts of other people.

Already at the crossing Jeff looked back and said, "Come on!"

Each gray hill crossed put them closer to the mountains. The bottoms were wider now, and once they crossed a half mile of meadow fed by a stream that made endless S turns in the sod. They saw their first cattle, far too many of them for the grass.

Then, one after another, they crossed meadows where streams ran slowly. There was water enough, but it could not touch enough land to help this range. The meadows ran out green, thinning to brown at the edges, then dying quickly against the hills. On the mountains ahead aspen parks reached up in long benches, and the eternal bluegreen of the pines and spruces said: Here is water and here is grass for all time.

In a narrow valley where cattle had cropped the grass ground level, Jeff stopped his sorrel. He pointed to where the silvery logs of aspens marked corrals and buildings backed against a hill at the head of the valley.

"Seven Cross," he said.

Jeff probably knew where Lone Star and Sash were too, for he had job-scouted yesterday, and he was one who learned much of a country in a short time.

Clay waited for him to speak, and Jeff knew that he was waiting. Early cold had put a flush on Jeff's pale cheeks, and now the sun was already turning the newly exposed skin the color of his brows and nose.

Jeff slouched in his saddle, looking all around, as if the country might throw enemies from behind every hill. When he knew that his son was not going to ask directions, Jeff made a tiny nod and rode up the valley.

For the first time in his life Clay was going toward a job alone. There was a quick lift of freedom about the thought, but still some part of him dragged after Jeff. It occurred to Clay that his father had not made any fuss about the split, if it could be called that.

After several minutes of studying the land ahead, Clay thought he knew where the main channels of the watershed came down. He could find Window Sash in time; it might take ten miles of extra riding for want of asking a question, but he would find the place.

Billy Nairn . . . a graying little feisty man, that's the way the name read.

Finding the ranch turned out easier than Clay expected. Sometime after noon he came into swampy ground where the wetness lay like the print of a hand pressed hard between the dead gray hills. There were a few cows with a Four Box brand, which would be Window Sash.

He followed along one finger of the swamp and came into a strong valley. Above him a low cross ridge crowned with aspens sprawled from hill to hill like a broken dam. There still were only a few cattle. Centuries of erosionary theft from the stark hills had laid three feet of rich soil in the bottom, and through it a stream moved slowly.

In the aspens on the ridge he met his first fence. After his hours of free riding the fence was a mild shock. The bark had not yet unrolled from the logs he removed to let his horse through. He saw the reason for the barrier then. The upper part of the valley had been allowed to go to hay. There must be six hundred acres of it, he estimated, lush native grasses so high the seeded heads were curling down.

The house was situated at the upper end of the valley, just before the hills pinched hard against the stream. From here the mountains appeared quite close. This must be the Sash, and it was a hay ranch. Briefly, Clay considered riding back to Seven Cross. Jeff would not say a word, even though he must have known about Sash.

All Clay had said to Vanita Krimble was, "I'll see."

After a moment, he rode toward the house.

The man was holding himself up with his elbows jammed between the corral rails. The position brought his hands close together on his chest and bent his back and gave him a huddled look. His face was bloody. His clothes were plastered with mud from the overflow of the water trough close to where the others stood.

The Honeywells were closest to him, pinning him against the fence. He had been thoroughly beaten, and now what expression there was left said that they would have to beat him some more.

"Who killed Andrews?" Anse Honeywell moved closer to the man against the bars.

"Hold it, Anse." The warning, not an order, came from a big fair-complexioned man who stood a little apart from the three others at the trough.

"I saw him come through the gate." Anse did not look around at Clay. With deadly patience he said to the beaten man, "Who did it, Kelley?"

Kelley's battered mouth worked slowly. "Go to hell," he mumbled. Primitive animal defiance took a little of the blankness from his face. He raised one hand defensively when Anse made a quick movement.

Anse caught the hand and jerked Kelley away from the rails with force that made the man's head snap back. Barr Honeywell's fists swung in long arcs that ended soddenly. Barr was scowling, but Anse viewed the beating with the air of a bloodless magistrate. There seemed to be no anger in Anse even when he kicked Kelley in the stomach when the man was lying, unmoving, on the ground.

"Maybe he didn't know," the blond man said, half angrily. "Kelley and Andrews were friends. They—"

"It's one nest up there at Krimble's. You'd better not

forget that, Nairn," Anse said.

The blond man was not the Billy Nairn that Clay had pictured. He was no older than Clay.

Barr rubbed his knuckles on his shirt. "Did anyone invite you to light down, Arbuckle?"

Barr's blood had risen while he was beating Kelley, and now he would try to let the heat carry him on to a bigger fight. Some men were like that, Clay thought; they needed just a little boost to get them over the hump of reluctance.

The Honeywells on the right, Anse being first. Nairn wore no pistol.

"This is still my place, Barr," Nairn said. He looked at Clay. "What do you want?"

"I'm Clay Arbuckle." Vanita should have told Nairn by now.

Apparently she had not, for the name meant nothing to Nairn. That was a jolt to Clay, completely out of proportion with the importance of the fact. He could not say that a woman had sent him here for a job. Even under the threat of Barr's intention, Clay had time to curse the fact that he had always been dependent on Jeff for words. Before these men, he couldn't even ask Nairn for a job.

"Anse and me know him," Barr said. "A tough. I wonder just how tough?"

Anse's deep-set eyes turned to Barr with a steady, quiet gaze, and Clay knew then that there would be no trouble. "You're sort of a fool at times, Barr," Anse said. "Come on, let's go home."

Anse strode away, not looking to see if his brother followed, but after a moment, Barr followed.

On the ground, Kelley moved one hand slowly and made gurgling noises deep in his throat, and then he was

48

quiet again. When the three men near the watering trough started toward their horses, a tubby, buck-toothed man wearing spectacles stopped before Nairn. He spread his hands. "Billy, I—" He looked over his shoulder at Kelley. "Oh, hell!" he said, as if that expressed all there was to say. He walked away.

Three of the horses that walked out of the yard wore different brands. The Honeywells were on Seven Cross mounts. Yesterday in town they had ridden unbranded horses.

"Do they own Seven Cross?" Clay asked.

"Sure." Nairn went over to Kelley, who was trying to push up on his elbows. He fell back with his face grinding into the mud. Frowning, worried, Nairn dipped his hat in the watering trough.

After a while Clay lent a hand. He and Nairn doused Kelley in the trough and got him on his feet. It was the first time Clay had ever touched a man to help him. When Kelley could move unaided he cursed both Nairn and Clay and staggered toward his horse.

He rode away slowly, hunched over the horn.

Nairn cursed vaguely, and then he remembered there was a stranger beside him. "What do you want?"

"I heard there was a job here."

"On this place?" Nairn's eyes dropped to Clay's pistol. "Who said so?"

Clay forced it out. "Jim Krimble's daughter."

Take the worry off Nairn's face and he would be a handsome man, maybe even a friendly man, Clay thought. "Come in and we'll see about it," Nairn said. All the way to the house he studied Clay from the sides of his eyes.

The Honeywells lost their last companion at the forks of
49

Boyer Creek. He was Allie Odom, the rounding, buck-toothed man, whose mouth was always in the semblance of a smile. He pushed his glasses up and down. He looked at his cattle along the stream, and at last he looked at Anse Honeywell.

"I didn't figure we'd get so mean with Art Kelley," Odom said. "I thought—"

"He was on your range, wasn't he?" Anse asked.

"There's been no trouble about that sort of thing before." Odom shook his head.

"Sam Andrews was never killed before. Think about that, Odom. You know I've always tried for the peaceful way out of this. I tried to lease range from Krimble for all of us, until grass comes back down here. Against my better judgment I listened to Tol Shepherd and Big George and went into that deal yesterday in South Fork."

Odom nodded.

"I was glad when it didn't come off," Anse said. "I hoped for peace up until Lone Star killed Sam. Maybe what we did today was a mistake. I don't like violence, Odom, but Krimble threw it at us. There isn't going to be any peace. Go home and think about it, Odom."

The Honeywells rode away. Barr said, "Gutless."

"And you may have too many for your own good, Barr. That young Arbuckle would have killed you in a second."

"The hell you say!"

They left a shower of dust behind them as they angled down a hill.

"Those two Arbuckles are just the same," Anse said. "We've got the old buck on our side, and I'll find a way to use the young one too."

"We should have killed him. We could have done it."

"I think so," Anse said.

"Why didn't we then?"

"For one thing, he would have killed me too. You see too short in front of your nose, Barr. You're remembering that young Arbuckle helped change our minds yesterday. You're remembering that he talked to Bitsy. Get your head up, Barr, and look beyond your nose."

They crossed a valley with a finger of water in it. At the top of the next hill Anse stopped and looked at the mountains. There would never be grass on the hills again. Let Odom and other fools think the grass would come back, but Anse knew better.

The patience of a lean buffalo wolf burned in his eyes as he looked upward. "There it is, Barr. There it lies, and we can do it."

Barr looked but his roots stayed in the hills. "That Krimble is tough."

"He *was* tough. He could be again, but his wife has got him toned down. He ain't the Jim Krimble that stole all of that up there, with Chaunce Wade's help. Wade ain't changed, but he's old. They can't hold all that with fifteen men. Ben Wavell may try to help him, but he'll be the only one.

Barr nodded absently. "These Arbuckles, Anse—"

"I'll handle them. They'll fit into my plans."

"You're always planning something big that depends too damned much on a lot of other things!"

Anse smiled. "Men get big that way."

"Yeah, hell! They starve too."

"Get your nose out of your shirt collar," Anse said. "Take a real honest look at all that." The sweep of Anse's hand covered twenty miles of mountains. "Why, man, there's grass for eternity up there! There's

51

everything—green parks five times as big as Nairn's hay field. There's winter shelter all along those low aspen ridges. It's never snow-locked solid along the lower edges. Why, even the timber up there will be worth a fortune someday, and—"

"I've been there," Barr said. "We should have taken that Arbuckle right there in the Horseshoe."

Anse Honeywell never let anger drive his thoughts in all directions; he used anger only for a purpose, so now he watched his brother patiently. Barr's thoughts would ran in a narrow channel until something caused Barr himself to change them.

They went on toward the Seven Cross.

"That young Arbuckle has a weak spot," Anse said. "It hurt him to see Kelley taking his beating. He didn't show it as much as Nairn, but I saw it just the same."

Barr grunted. "I didn't see nothing but his dead cold face. We should have—"

"I doubt we'll have to watch him as close as someone else."

"His father?"

"Nairn."

Barr scowled. "Nairn's all right. We know he's got to be on our side."

"Nairn's been riding up to Lone Star quite a bit, I hear. I see him following Vanita Krimble around like a pup at the Comanche schoolhouse dance last month. Now I'm wondering how young Arbuckle wound up at Sash looking for a job. If I thought she talked alone to Arbuckle in town yesterday . . ."

"We had him dead to right, the bunch of us," Barr said. He was speaking again of Clay Arbuckle.

Anse did not hear. His mind was busy tailoring situations to suit a purpose. He was sure that one man, moving hard toward a goal, could pull into his traction fifty other men to help him along.

Three rough-coated dogs, blunt in the heads, wide of shoulders, came low across the grass to greet the Honeywells when they approached Seven Cross.

"Como, Bull, Champ! Quiet, you hammerheads," Anse said, almost fondly. "Fall in there!"

The dogs stopped barking. They moved to the left side of the horses and trotted into the yard with the brothers.

The building of Seven Cross belied the limited acreage of the valley range and the dead hills all around. The chinking was tight between the aspen logs, the roofs in good repair. There was no litter in the yard. The corrals were sound. It was mostly Barr's work, but Anse took pride in it.

A wisp of a woman in a deep sunbonnet and a black merino dress was sitting in a rocker on the porch of the ranchhouse. Her eyes were listless as she watched Anse swing down. Barr leaned over to take the loose reins and lead the horse toward the corral.

For a few moments Anse stood in the yard, stretching saddle kinks out of his legs. He liked the solid neatness of Seven Cross. Each return to it always soothed a gnawing feeling engendered by seeing the larger possessions of other men. He stamped his feet absently, looking toward the mountains, and his mind multiplied the ground he stood on by a hundred. A thousand, he thought, would be more like it. Those who helped him would hang on for a while when he made the big move, but in the end it would be Anse Honeywell alone.

Barr could have Seven Cross; Barr would be content with that much. The old woman, who understood Anse too well, would not want to move from Seven Cross.

"You should have gone to the burying, Anse." Mrs. Honeywell's voice dragged with the slowness of her Tennessee hill country heritage. "Barr figured to."

Anse stopped to scratch Champ behind the ears. The other two dogs crowded in to get their share.

"We had business, Ma."

"Sam Andrews helped your pa get started here. You were riding with Sam when he got shot. Barr spoke of going to the burying, Anse."

She was the only person in the world who could irritate Anse. She must know it, he thought. Her accusations were always roundabout, and they always dragged in the fact that he was handling Barr.

"Did a man show up here today?" Anse's view of the corral was partly blocked by a stable.

"It was a good burying, Anse. You should have been there, you and Barr." Mrs. Honeywell moved her rocker slowly. Against the age of her face her jet-black eyes were penetrating and alive. "He's here. What for, Anse?"

"Where is he?"

"He ain't an obliging man, Anse. He taken care of the buggy team for me without no asking, but still he ain't an obliging man a-tall." Mrs. Honeywell rocked a few times. "He was near the corral a while back."

Anse started away.

"What for did you hire that man, Anse?"

Among other things, the continual use of his name by his mother bothered Anse. He kept walking.

"There's something wrong inside that man, Anse. Against him, Sam Andrews is still alive and laughing."

She might be right, in her superstitious way. There was ice and frozen blood inside old Jeff. Unlike his son, Jeff never would have batted an eye at the sight of a

54

beaten man on the ground. Anse was sure that Jeff had hired on here for some personal reason, for all men moved because of self alone.

Barr and Jeff were standing at the corner of the corral. Barr's methods of sounding out a man were limited, and his patience in the matter short; so now he was puzzled, and also a little afraid. He was like tough old Bull backing off from a timber wolf, allowing fear but unwilling to show it.

Anse said nothing. He rolled a cigarette, taking lots of time, raising his eyes to Jeff's face between the little motions. Jeff waited, undisturbed.

He had been bearded yesterday when he came early to Seven Cross, inquiring about work. Anse had not hired him then, and Jeff had said he would ride on to some of the other ranches. He must have found out plenty about the trouble before he met Anse and Barr returning from their second trip to town. It was then Anse hired him. Anse wondered now why the beard was gone.

"Any news about Andrews?" Anse asked.

Jeff shook his head.

Last night Allie Odom had come by to say that Wavell found nothing on the ridge above Little Squaw. The sheriff had gone to Lone Star then. He would try, Anse thought, but it did not matter to Anse whether Wavell ever found out what Lone Star rider had killed Sam Andrews.

Anse said, "Your boy is over at Sash."

"Uh-huh."

"How come?" Barr was belligerent. "Anse said last night we could use you both."

"My boy thinks he likes haying better than some other things," Jeff said.

55

"Yeah? Well, he's working for a man that's sort of friendly toward Jim Krimble," Barr said.

Anse caught a deep-lying glint of something violent in Jeff's eyes when Krimble's name was spoken. There was a cross wind moving through the scene. Jeff looked at Barr and said nothing. It would be well, in time, to know just what Jeff wanted from the fight, but for the moment Anse was satisfied. Jeff hated Jim Krimble; the hill ranchers merely wanted to take something from Krimble. Hate was better. Whatever Jeff's long range interests were, the grim old tough-mouth was another pistol on Anse's side.

"Let's go find something to eat," Anse said.

They walked to the house together. Anse knew that Barr was not satisfied with Jeff, for the old man was Clay's father, and Barr would never be happy about either of them until in some way he closed the circuit on what had happened in the Horseshoe, first, and then at Nairn's.

Let Barr fret over such small parts of the affair.

"Barr," Amanda Honeywell drawled, as Anse and Jeff went inside.

Barr turned away from the door. "What, Ma?"

"What's that man's name?"

"Jeff Arbuckle."

The old woman rocked. "That's a good name, Barr. He ain't though. He's killer-bad, Barr."

Barr knew it, and he was worried. He wanted an ally, someone with whom he could discuss his brother's high-handed mistakes and wild dreams, without any idea of doing anything to change them. He wanted a sounding board, but he could not talk to a woman, not even his mother.

"And Anse is worse than killer-bad, Barr." The

woman's voice was sterile with judgment. It made her oldest son uneasy.

"He knows what he's doing," Barr said.

Mrs. Honeywell was looking down the valley. "Your Pa talked some of raising crops here, Barr."

Barr had talked of it too, even before the dry years, but each time he mentioned crops, Anse had made his little smile and held out his hands. "They won't fit a plough handle. Will yours, Barr?"

"This is cattle country, Ma."

"It was. Billy Nairn is raising hay, Barr."

"He can't sell it."

"What's needed will sell."

Barr started into the house. There was no use arguing with his mother when she got her mind set.

"You'd best let Anse go his way alone, Barr. He's headed down the devil's road."

Clay let Billy Nairn run on. "Just leave the average man alone and he'll spill everything he knows in ten minutes," Jeff always said.

One end of the Sash ranchhouse was living quarters and the other part was kitchen. The bunkhouse was empty. Nairn had explained that when he cut his herd to almost nothing last spring, his last rider had gone to work for. Lone Star. It did not seem to Clay that Nairn held any grudge against Jim Krimble because the man owned the only adequate range in the country.

Clay sat at the kitchen table and watched Nairn throw his restlessness around the room. Nairn talked of everything but the subject that must be worrying him most of all: what would Krimble do about Kelley?

"In a few weeks I'll need a pretty good sized hay crew, sure enough." Nairn stared out the window. The small panes were dusty and the corners were rounding in with spider webs. Clay thought of Dutch Holcomb's sparkling windows, and then, quite naturally, he thought of Bitsy Miller and wondered where she was.

It was not like Clay to let his mind stray when there was a man to watch and study; but for once he guessed it did not matter.

"Vanita said there might be a job here, huh?"

Clay nodded. Nairn wanted to know just how directly Vanita had acted. Let him ask then.

"She just said there might be work here?"

"A riding job," Clay said.

Nairn was a powerful man. He was young. On a peg near his bed hung a pistol belt he must have worn sometime. Clay considered those facts, and he considered the man's indecision. Without a pistol a man was harder to judge, but Nairn was a left-sider, all right. Probably he was a terrible-tempered fighter with his fists.

It was Jeff's contention that a man was a fool to fight with his fists, or to fight at all, unless it was to kill.

"Stay overnight, anyway," Nairn said. "We'll see about the job."

He could not make his mind up cleanly. He wanted to talk to Vanita about Clay, and maybe he wanted a little backing when Lone Star came riding to ask questions about Kelley. On the basis of that Nairn shouldn't stack so high as a man, Clay thought; but still, in spite of the man's fretting, Clay sort of liked him.

Perhaps it was because Clay seldom had been given a chance to like anyone—or to dislike anyone.

Nairn kicked a blackened log end into the dead fireplace. "You know cattle, Arbuckle?"

Clay nodded.

Nairn was doubtful about that. He looked at Clay's pistol, and then at Clay's wooden expression. "Of course, I *will* need a hay crew."

Nairn kept the door open until dark, glancing westward frequently, toward the mountains, toward Lone Star. A chill rolled in with dusk; Sash was considerably higher than South Fork, Clay thought. He watched Nairn build a fire in the fireplace.

Vanita Krimble rode into the yard an hour after dark. Nairn raced across the room to open the door when she hailed the house. He would have talked to her in the yard, but Clay heard her say, "Don't be an old woman, Billy," and then she came inside.

Once in Granada Clay had seen a dancehall girl wearing levis. Now he stared at Vanita in a man's outfit. She was no dancehall fly-up-the-crick, he knew; there must be a good many things he did not know.

The firelight touched her high cheekbones and ran a golden tone along her brow when she crossed the room to where Clay was sitting by the fireplace. A man could lose himself in her eyes, Clay thought.

"I'm glad you made it, Mr. Arbuckle."

Nairn was scowling about something. "He says you said there might be a job here, Nita."

She looked from Clay to Nairn, and Clay saw that it took her but an instant to understand that he and Nairn had not talked bluntly to each other. "I said you might need a man here, Billy. You do, don't you?" It was not really a question.

"Well—" Nairn said.

"You know you do," Vanita said. That settled it as far as she was concerned. "My father will be over tomorrow to talk about Art Kelley. What happened?"

"The Honeywells and some others picked him up on

59

his way to Andrews' funeral. They brought him over here to work on him, so's it would tie me into the thing. I didn't want any part of it."

"Why didn't you stop it then?" Vanita asked.

Nairn turned white. A coward would have turned red and would have made excuses. Clay felt a small tug of obligation to Nairn. "It would have been pretty hard to stop," Clay said.

Vanita looked at him thoughtfully. Her interest threw a warmth over him, loosening some part of the tightness and loneliness that had always been a part of his life. She glanced at Nairn, and she might have been comparing the two of them.

"What did your father say?" Nairn asked.

"I wasn't home to hear him. He's coming here tomorrow, and then he's going to Seven Cross. Keep your head, Billy."

That was what she had come to say, Clay knew.

Nairn and the girl went out together. Clay heard them talking in the yard a few moments later, and then her horse walked into the night and Nairn returned. He stood large in the middle of the floor with his shadow a great blotch on the wall behind him. He studied Clay through narrowed eyes.

"I guess I can use you, Arbuckle."

The reason for his finally making up his mind was gnawing at him because he knew that Clay knew also what the reason was. "Don't you ever stand up when a lady comes into the room, Arbuckle?"

Clay thought a moment. "Should have," he said.

He turned in across the room from Nairn. Out on the gray hills coyotes talked to him. In a way, the Sash was something like the wheat valley. It was wrong, he sensed, to try to go back to boyhood, but for the moment there was nothing wrong in thinking that he had found in one place some of the peace of another place he had known long before.

Old Jeff's tough mouth and bitter eyes would not be there above him in the morning. Jeff was at Seven Cross with the Honeywells. All of them sort of belonged together over there.

And maybe Clay belonged with left-siders like Billy Nairn. It was a startling thought, so pleasant Clay could not trust the credibility of it.

There were four of them from Lone Star the next morning. They came out of the aspens above the house and rode along the hill before they turned straight down toward the buildings. The dust from their horses drifted slowly toward the hayfield.

In the blacksmith shop, where they were sharpening mower teeth, Clay and Nairn laid down their tools. Nairn was nervous but he was not afraid. Clay went outside with him, wondering how a jumpy man could be without fear; but that was the way it was with Nairn. Maybe the lack of a pistol had something to do with it.

They came into the yard four abreast, Jim Krimble and Chauncey Wade in the middle, flanked by two cowboys. The short gun scabbards of the cowboys wagged a little when they brought their horses to a halt.

In the guarded expressions of the two flankers, rather than from Krimble and Wade, Clay saw that this was a war party. They were ready to start here if the questions they would ask did not receive the proper answers.

Jim Krimble ignored Clay. The dark, jowly face was set on Nairn. Chauncey Wade watched Clay, and nothing else.

"What happened, Nairn?" Krimble asked.

"They brought him here, that's all." Nairn was no

longer nervous.

"Why?"

"To tie me into it."

"Did they need to do that?" Krimble asked.

Nairn pointed toward the hay field. "How many cows do you see down there now?"

Krimble did not look. "I've thought of that, Nairn. But your friends are still hill ranchers. Where do you stand?"

"With Sash."

"Just Sash, huh?"

"That's all."

"Suppose there's more passes made to tie you into it?"

"There will be," Nairn said. "But Kelley was the last man from either side that will be brought here for a beating."

"Yeah." It was only a vague word, for Krimble's mind was ploughing into something ahead. He looked hard at Clay, disliking him and showing it. "I thought you wanted hay hands, Nairn."

"He is," Nairn said.

Krimble's fleshy face was dark with doubt. "I could say different. Suppose I said I didn't want a pistolman in my front yard?"

Nairn shook his head. "It's not quite your front yard, Jim. This is Sash."

Clay watched Chauncey Wade for the little signs that would tell what Clay could not read from Krimble's voice and face. There was a mobility about the foreman's countenance that was lacking on Krimble's blunt features; and now Wade might have been just slightly amused. From that Clay decided Krimble was feeling, not pushing.

"I see." Krimble nodded. "Your word has always been good with me, Nairn. About your friends down here—"

"That's another matter," Nairn said.

"And a mean one too," Krimble said. "You'll find you have to fight harder to straddle a thing like this than you do if you're on one side or the other."

He sounded like Jeff, Clay thought.

"That may be," Nairn said.

Krimble looked at the hay field. "I could use all that at Lone Star this winter. Come up and talk about it, if you care to, Nairn."

"I will." Nairn nodded.

Chauncey Wade looked back at Clay as the Lone Star men rode away. They went in the general direction of Seven Cross. Jeff was over there; it worried Clay. The Honeywells would not back down on their own land, and Jeff was working for them.

Clay tried to determine what he owed his father. There was no affection between them, and never had been. The father and son relationship had started too late in Jeff's life, and with too much of a jar, to create an obligation for its own sake. They had given nothing to each other but their presence.

"I'm in the middle for fair now." Nairn was frowning at the ground. "Krimble pushed me around."

"I didn't notice it," Clay said.

Nairn's features brightened slowly. He was a man who needed boosting now and then, Clay thought, a man who went from happiness to gloom easily.

"Maybe I did stand up to Krimble," Nairn said. "He was right about straddling, but what can a man do? The hills will never be cattle range again in our time. I'm the only one that's tried to do anything different. When I

63

sell my hay to Krimble, the others will say I'm siding with him.

"They'll just sit down here and starve, or else let Anse Honeywell lead 'em into a fool's fight to break into Lone Star range. I meant what I said, Arbuckle. It's Sash with me, and that's all."

That fitted in a general way with Jeff's ideas, but still there was something different. It came to Clay that he had taken a lot of statements from Jeff and had tried to direct his life by them, as one would follow the blaze marks of a trail. And now, although the statements still seemed as sound as a bullet, there was something wrong with them.

"Get the fire going again, will you?" Nairn strode away toward the house. When he returned he was wearing a pistol. It bothered him all morning. He kept hitching at it, touching it. He was like a man running his tongue into the cavity of a freshly pulled tooth.

They worked over the mowing machine that Nairn had bought in South Fork, a beaten contraption that the Army had discarded years before. In the shank of the afternoon they tried it on tough-stemmed grass. It clattered and wobbled, but it worked. It needed at least another day's labor, and then it would probably fall apart a few times under serious stress.

When the hills were losing the last of sunset's shadows, they racked their tools in the blacksmith shop. Before they went to the house they walked around the mower, touching parts here and there.

There was a feeling of pride in what they had done, and it sort of bound them toward each other. Clay could not understand why it was that he liked Billy Nairn a little better than he had that morning. A busted-up old mowing machine that they had hammered and pounded at . . . Jeff would say in his biting voice, "What are you, a stinking farmer at heart?"

"I'm not much of a cook—maybe you've already noticed," Nairn said, "but I think we'll get along."

"Sure," Clay said. That was as close as he had come to reaching out toward friendship in a long time. "Sure we will," he said. That sounded a little better.

He took a last look at the hay field before he followed Nairn toward the house. Before Clay reached the woodpile he was wondering how Vanita planned to have him aid her father by working at Sash. She might as well have been looking directly at his pistol when she insisted that it was a riding job.

He wondered, too, what had happened at Seven Cross that day.

If there were no trouble in the country Clay thought that right here at Sash he could begin to find some of the satisfaction that he suspected there was in living. He wanted to be able to look at Nairn and think, "We share work and food and friendship. I am going to help him cut his first crop of hay with a rickety old mower."

It was not much to want to think that instead of, "He's a left-sider. I could let him draw clear, and then kill him easily."

Anse Honeywell came into the cold morning with a feeling of accomplishment. He had included the probable action of adversaries in the laying of his plans, and the structure was stronger thereby.

Today Jim Krimble would make his contribution.

The slant of the sun was yet no lower than the tops of the mountains. The valley and the hills appeared chilled and tired by the long wait through darkness, but that had no effect on Anse. Some men were sour before

65

breakfast; he was at his best then, and if he missed breakfast it did not matter at all.

He heard his brother banging buckets at the hill spring. Nothing about early morning ever pleased Barr. Down the yard, Jeff Arbuckle came out of the bunkhouse and looked around him like a cat on strange ground. Bull and Como and Champ loped up from the corral to greet Anse.

He patted their heads, and kept staring at Jeff. The old man's face was bright from shaving, but there was no smoke from the bunkhouse stove pipe. The old trapmouth had shaved with cold water!

The small detail annoyed Anse. He was a man who prided himself on disregarding unimportant things, but over there was a man who had gone him one better. Shaving with cold water when he did not have to. The old hellion was a savage!

Mrs. Honeywell called from the kitchen, "I need wood."

"Barr will get it in a minute," Anse said. The petty annoyance of a moment before vanished with the words. He looked at the mountains, now caught in the first flood-light of day. With the vision of a king Anse Honeywell's deep eyes saw what he wanted to see, and the day was his to bend and twist as he desired.

The affair was shaping up nicely. Right from the start it had been blessed with luck. If the showdown in South Fork had gone through, with Krimble and Wade being wiped out, there would have been a strong taste in the country's mouth. Anse prized the good will of his fellow men because good will was useful.

When both sides were shot up and weary of the fight, it would be a simpler matter to emerge from the wreckage and stand high on the mountains as a strong

66

man bringing peace. Anse was quite sure that men who fought without thinking ahead also were likely to make peace without thinking ahead.

Eventually, after it was done, the hill ranchers would recognize that they were right where they had been before, maybe worse off. But by then there would not be so many of them to give trouble. One by one Anse would be able to shake them loose from any ambitions they had to share the mountains with him.

He realized the ground he must cross was shaky, but by careful stepping from hummock to hummock, by always planning far ahead, he would get where he was going while idiots like Callaway rushed in and sank.

The weight was now on Lone Star because Lone Star had killed Andrews. Anse was without guilt. Slapping Kelley around was no crime, nothing at all, but Jim Krimble must come riding about the matter.

Krimble would come ready to fight if a fight was offered. There was going to be none. Dragging at Krimble's purpose was the knowledge that one of his riders had killed a hill rancher from ambush. Anse smiled; it was hell how a fair man was forced to consider such items.

What could he do here in the yard at Seven Cross? Carrying in the back of his mind the fact that there was guilt on his side, with no fight offered, the best Krimble could do was talk. Then he would leave, and soon the country would magnify the fact that Jim Krimble had done nothing at all about Art Kelley. Krimble had a position to maintain. Get around him two or three times and then all the savageness in him that had been sublimated since his marriage would explode.

Afterward, in the eyes of the country, it would be he who had started the fight. That was much the best way.

Already Anse had taken advantage of the first Lone Star mistake, the killing of Andrews. He had reported it to Wavell.

Anse was proud of his shrewdness in looking into the minds of others; but he never banked entirely on the skill. The way things would be set up here at Seven Cross, Krimble couldn't do any damage if he did let his temper get away.

They came straight up the valley, not hurrying, riding like honest men with business to attend to. That's what they were, too; it made Anse smile. When he saw that the two with Krimble and Wade were, indeed, Jack Bovee and Toby Lashbrook, he was further pleased because of the accuracy of his anticipation.

Anse waited in the yard unarmed. Krimble knew full well that Anse feared no man, so the lack of a pistol could not be called cowardice. Plan strongly, cleverly, and all the little happen-chances leap up in your favor.

With two words Anse restrained the dogs when they would have streaked down the valley to meet the riders.

They came in four abreast, wide-spaced for trouble. When they entered the yard the two men on the flanks dropped back a little.

Old Wade's Roman nose and icy eyes poked in every direction, toward the house, the outbuildings, the silent, waiting barn where Barr and Jeff were lying in the haymow.

"Women in the house, Jim," he murmured.

Another of Krimble's weaknesses; Anse should have thought long ago of a way to thrust at that soft spot.

"Art Kelley is in one hell of a shape this morning, Honeywell," Krimble said.

"Sam Andrews is dead."

68

Krimble's voice came as evenly as a carpet being unrolled slowly. "Art was on his way to the funeral. He worked for Sam a long time before he came to my place. Him and Sam were friends. You knew all that, Honeywell."

That much wasted on truth and logic. Anse waited.

"Nobody from my place killed Andrews," Krimble said.

Anse looked at the mountains with an air of patience that said he could bear up under any kind of lies. It pleased him to see that Krimble's face was darker when the moment passed.

"Get down and have some coffee, Krimble. I'm ready to listen to anything reasonable you have to say."

A truly clever man would have accepted, but Anse banked on his knowledge of Krimble. He saw the insult strike as calculated. He saw the mental bunching around the wound.

Krimble said, "I'll get down."

He swung off his horse and unstrapped his pistol belt and let it fall. He was on the left side of his horse, shielded by it from the weapons in the hayloft. Anse moved down the yard, so that Krimble had to come around his mount. Deliberately, Krimble moved toward Anse.

There was fat on the man. He would be grunting and winded in a few minutes. Anse could move quickly. He was sure of the power that lay in his huge wrists and stooped shoulders. If he stayed clear of Krimble during the first few flurries, he could then step in and beat Krimble raw.

Anse was tempted, but he shook his head. "You're an old man, Krimble. I don't beat up fat old men. Better take him away, Wade. I don't want to hurt him, and I can't be responsible for what the dogs might do to him."

"Don't fret about the dogs none at all," Wade said.

The implication pulled a trigger of cold fury in Anse Honeywell. To think that anyone could talk so calmly about shooting Bull or Champ or Como . . . It unseated the control of which Anse was so proud.

He was eager then to pound Jim Krimble senseless. "Hike for the barn!" he called to the dogs, and he did not need to look to know they were obeying.

His face happy with a fighter's light, Krimble was moving slower now, closing the little distance that was left.

The blast of gunpowder in the haymow jerked at nerves and muscles. Bovee went for his pistol. Wade's voice was a sharp crack. "Hold it, Bovee!"

In the dust just ahead of Krimble the bullet had made a sput and flicked away. Krimble took another step and there was another sput of dust near his feet. He stopped.

Anger cleared from Anse's mind in an instant, and he took quick advantage of an unplanned factor. "I knew you'd try to make an idiot of yourself, Krimble. I told Barr to warn you off."

Wade said, "That wasn't Barr's .44-40."

The threats that an ordinary man would have spoken were all on Krimble's face as he stared at Anse. He still might have stepped ahead, but Wade repeated his warning sharply.

"That isn't Barr up there!"

Krimble turned slowly and went back to his horse.

In the loft, flat in the hay, Jeff stared along the barrel of his carbine. His face was wild. He had broken the rim of a rotting tooth by clenching his jaws so hard, and now he continued to grind his teeth against the stab of the broken molar.

Krimble's face was the same; it could never change because Jeff's last remembrance of it had corroded into something that could not be altered. It was the same down there in the yard as it had been on the foggy morning when Jim Krimble stood over Jeff with a smoking pistol. "He's dying," Krimble had said. "Damn his soul! He got out of it easy!"

Remembrance was a compressing wave of madness. Long ago Jeff thought he had tamed his rage to serve him against the day he found Krimble again, but now the pits of hell were popping and all the years of savage planning were forgotten.

The sound of his own carbine had been a crash in Jeffs brain, sweeping away cold sanity. He had been all right until after he put the two shots in front of Krimble to keep the man from being beaten. No one but Jeff had a right to touch Krimble. No one down there, except Chauncey Wade, could even guess what was due Jim Krimble. That was logic which must be allowed to hold. Krimble was leaving now, and he must go unharmed.

But no logic could stand against remembering fed by years of corrosive brooding. Krimble was riding away, and it was as if he were going once again into the fog, into the years.

Jeff put his sights on Krimble's back, careful not to center on the spine where death would be quick, but lining instead a few inches to the left. That was it, and now there was nothing left but a steady press against the curving warmth of the trigger.

It was wrong; it was not the proper vengeance, and it would wreck a lifetime of planning. That much came through the hot skin-tightened feel of madness clamping Jeff's head. He knew he was not whole at the moment. He knew he must do something, or break apart entirely.

71

The last rider leaving the yard was slender Jack Bovee. He turned to look toward the hayloft and the casual movement in the saddle slid his right arm near his pistol.

Jeff moved his carbine just a trifle. He shot Bovee through the chest, from side to side. The horse made a startled jump, and then it stopped and swung around when the reins struck the ground. Bovee was lying still.

The Lone Star men spun their horses. Their pistols were coming clear when Anse called, "There's seven riflemen up there, Krimble!"

Lone Star did not know; they could not know. Jeff watched their anger fade to caution, and he watched Anse Honeywell stand unafraid in the yard. Jeff was all right now. He glanced at Barr. For just an instant Barr returned a look of horror and then he put his attention on covering Krimble.

"He went for his pistol, Krimble," Anse said. "You know how hot-headed he always was."

Krimble swung down and went over to Bovee. He knelt for a few moments and then he came up tall like an Indian and gray-faced. "You're a dirty damned liar, Honeywell, and you know it."

"You weren't looking," Anse said. "He went for his pistol. You came for trouble and you got it, and that's the way it's going to stand with the country." He turned his back on Krimble and walked away.

By the time Lone Star rode away with Bovee lashed across the saddle, Anse had smoothed out most of the lump created in his mind by the sudden action. Bovee had drawn, or started to draw, to kill Anse. Anse had been unarmed. The score was even now, Bovee for Andrews, but the hill ranchers must not be allowed to let that attitude drop them into inertia.

72

Anse frowned. He called the dogs from the barn. They came leaping across the yard, then skidded around to sniff at the blood where Bovee had fallen. They walked away from the spot stiff-legged and came to Anse, who patted them absently while he tried to figure out why Jeff had shot Jack Bovee.

Maybe the old cuss was trigger-crazy, but he did not look it.

Amanda Honeywell was still standing on the porch. Anse looked at her. "You saw him try to draw, didn't you?"

Mrs. Honeywell looked accusingly at Anse. "That man didn't try to draw no pistol, Anse. You know he didn't."

"Yes he did. You just weren't looking, Ma."

"I was looking," the old woman drawled. "You're going up the devil's road, Anse Honeywell. I was looking."

Barr and Jeff came out of the barn, and Anse walked across the yard. He kicked dust toward the blood when he passed it, and he spoke sharply to the dogs when they stopped to sniff.

Things upset Barr, Anse thought. The old woman had pounded at least some of her teachings into him, and now Barr was looking at Jeff with fear and revulsion. Jeff's face was as cold as ever. It bothered Anse, for he liked to know what was in a man's mind.

"What for?" Anse asked.

"He started to draw," Jeff said.

"Oh, hell—"

"You said so yourself, didn't you?" Jeff asked.

Anse mulled it over, and then he began to smile. He and Jeff would get along all right, as long as the old tough did not develop too many ambitions of his own.

73

Barr gave them both an odd look and then he went toward the house. Mrs. Honeywell was coming out with a broom. "Get me an old shovel, Barr," she ordered. "We'll clean the top away, but blood from murder goes all the way to the center of the earth."

She spoke loudly so Anse would hear. The creepy old witch, he thought. Why was it she could irritate him? Jeff did not seem to mind. His face was cold, and the listening silence was there like something coiled.

Anse looked at the mountains. After a while his thoughts were moving smoothly again.

For three days Sheriff Ben Wavell had been at Sash, helping with the cutting of the hay. He said he had nothing else to do. There had not been enough sign on the ridge above Little Squaw crossing for an Apache to read, so the killing of Sam Andrews would have to ride along unsolved for a while.

Wavell had been at Allie Odom's place when he heard the news of Bovee's death. He had gone at once to Seven Cross, and then to Lone Star, and later he talked to Amanda Honeywell. He said the result of his investigation was inconclusive: Krimble and Wade did not know whether Bovee had started to draw or not. When they had gone back to him on the ground, his pistol was still holstered.

Clay could not believe the sheriff had let down. In spite of Wavell's chatter and easy ways, there was a deep running quality in the man. He and Jeff were alike in one respect: a persistence flowing powerfully. Someday, Clay thought, he would have someone besides Jeff as an anchor of comparison.

Vanita Krimble came riding in just after supper. Wavell went out to meet her and when he brought her into the house, Clay saw her eyes move purposefully around the room until she found him, and then she smiled.

Some inner excitement ran through Clay, and he knew he lacked foundation to judge it properly. His name, when it came from her in greeting, took new significance; it was not a handle to be used, but a bond between them.

She disturbed some unused part of Clay's responses, some part that had never been touched in his experiences with other women.

"Where's Billy?" she asked.

Clay pulled a chair from before the fireplace. He brushed a wisp of hay from the seat and held the chair while Vanita sat down. Wavell's gaze moved between the two of them thoughtfully.

"He went to South Fork to hire hands," Wavell said.

"He won't get many," Vanita said. "The Honeywells have been to town, and the word is out that anyone helping put up hay for Lone Star is siding against the hills."

"Uh-huh," Wavell said vaguely. "Didn't Billy tell you he was going in today—when he was at your place the other evening?"

"You're a busybody, Ben. Of course I didn't know, or I wouldn't have asked."

"Sure." Wavell sat down, stretching his legs to a resting place on a rawhide chair.

Vanita said, "My bay loosened a shoe on the way down. I wonder if—"

"Sure. Clay will look at it. Show him which foot it is," Wavell said.

"You *are* a busybody, Ben."

"Yep. An old tired busybody." There was no banter in

75

Wavell's tone. "Go ahead, Clay."

Out in the dusk Vanita caught the reins of the brockled bay and towed the animal out of earshot of the house, watching Clay as he walked beside her.

"That's your father over at Seven Cross, isn't it?"

"Yes.

"He's the one that shot Jack Bovee."

There was no comment needed, Clay thought.

"Why did he go to work for the Honeywells?"

"I don't know," Clay answered.

"He could have come here. I told you—"

"He already had the job when you talked to me."

"I see," Vanita said. They were close together in the dusk. "There's two men dead already. This will be a nasty fight, Clay—if it's allowed to go on. It could be stopped so easily."

"How?"

"The Honeywells. With them out of it, the other hill men would mill around a while and then settle down."

"Getting rid of the Honeywells would take some doing."

"You could do it."

"I could, yes—" Clay gave her a startled look.

"It would be worth five hundred dollars."

There it was, flat and simple. "Who sent you?"

"Nobody. But don't worry about that. I can get the money overnight."

"Not for me." Something that had just started to heal in Clay was wrenched loose again. There was a bitter taste to his thoughts.

"A thousand?" Vanita asked.

"You came to the wrong man."

"Not for any price?"

"No."

Her manner changed abruptly. Her breath came out in a long sigh, and her voice was without quick directness when she said, "I'm glad I was right. My father says you're in this for money, a pistol to be bought. For a while I was worried after I told you to come here. If I could have bought you, anybody else could have done the same. Lone Star has so few friends, Clay, that I had to be sure about you.

"I told you you could help my father by coming here, but that wasn't the truth. I was worried to death about Billy, but now I know he'll be all right." She touched him lightly on the arm and his muscles jerked involuntarily.

"How much are you worried about Billy? I mean—"

"He's a friend. Help me up, please."

Clay was awkward and he knew it. He gripped her arm too tightly, and he put too much energy into his boost. Her teeth were a soft white streak in the dusk as she smiled at him from the saddle. She leaned toward him, looking down.

"Clay—"

"Yes?"

"You've never been to Lone Star, have you?"

"You know I haven't."

"Well? I'd say this weather was going to hold. You'll get the hay in, all right, and by tomorrow afternoon, Billy ought to be able to spare you for a while."

Clay thought it over. "Your father—"

"He's probably away, but even if he isn't, any guest is welcome at Lone Star." She smiled again suddenly. "You're not afraid to ride with me, are you?"

"All right. I'll tell Billy."

"Good night, Clay."

There were no dark thoughts in his mind now. He

listened to the bay walking toward the hills, and then he strode toward the house. If he had been a singing man or a whistling man he would have expressed himself.

At Allie Odom's Quarter Circle twenty odd men were waiting near the corral when the Honeywells rode in. The ranchers were lounging against the gray rails, or squatting, toying with bits of earth and pebbles. It pleased Anse to know they had been waiting for him. It displeased him because there were not forty men here. The difference indicated how smoothly Wavell had been working.

Mrs. Odom quartered away from the back door of the house with a basket of washing. Anse swung down and touched his hat and spoke pleasantly to her. She nodded curtly. Anse smiled. Women were bound to the trifling details of life, burdened too much with what they owned, always wanting more, but afraid to go after it.

There would be some women-minded men among the group at the corral also, thanks largely to Ben Wavell.

Odom was nervous. He was unhappy about the meeting being called at Circle, and that was why Anse had insisted that it be here.

"Let's get started," Odom said. "This is about all that's going to show up, I guess."

Big George Callaway growled, "The Gentle Annies will show up about the time the fight is all our way. To hell with any range for them then."

"I feel the same," Anse said. "But I believe, as far as we can, we should avoid a murderous fight. It's clear that Krimble won't compromise of his own free will, so maybe we can force a compromise."

Grizzled Olin Limberis said, "That's mighty interesting, Anse, but I didn't come here to hear that kind of talk. What else you got to say?"

"I suggest that we gather a thousand head of cattle and drive them to the meadows at the head of Lost Creek. They'll spread out like prairie fire. Then we'll drop down to the south end of the mountains and put another thousand head in at Big Spruce hogback. Then we'll see what happens."

Tol Shepherd pulled a splinter from a rail and chewed it. "Where's Krimble all this time?"

"He's got fifteen men and twenty miles of mountains. If he pushes our cows out at one place, we'll be putting them back at another," Anse said. "He'll soon be tired of that."

"It ain't direct," Big George said. "We could go right in at Lone Star and settle things fast."

"We could stick our necks in a bear trap too," Anse said. "Who wants to be the first man killed? I tell you we can plague Krimble to death by doing things my way."

Big George said, "It ain't direct."

Fred Geldien was a short-coupled man with a bristling shock of red hair and a stubborn mouth. Not yet thirty, he had seven children. "It ain't nothing," he said. "Callaway talks fights and you, Honeywell, try to talk around it. At least Big George is honest."

"You mean I ain't?" Anse asked.

"I mean no one puts cows on Krimble's land without a shooting fight, and you know it. A half dozen more graves in these valleys won't settle anything."

Odom was nodding eagerly.

"What's your suggestion, Geldien?" Anse asked.

"I'm unloading what cows I got left and plowing my valley land to wheat. Ben Wavell is right."

"Why did you bother to ride over?" Anse asked.

79

"To see if anybody had a sensible idea," Geldien answered. "So far there ain't been no sense talked."

"Except now, of course," Anse said mildly. "We all turn farmers, huh, Geldien?"

"We all suit ourselves," Geldien said. "I'd run cows, if I had my ruthers about it, but I'm not barreling into any scrap that will smoke up the whole country and settle nothing."

"Has it occurred to you, Geldien, that Krimble controls all the water that comes into these hills?" Anse asked.

"Maybe it did, before you even thought of it," Geldien said. "Krimble gave his promise not to monkey with a drop of that water."

Terry Latham, another family man, spoke up. "That's right. Ben Wavell passed it on to us."

Odom nodded. "That's a fact, Anse. I've been thinking some of doing like Billy Nairn."

Damn Ben Wavell and his meddling. Anse had overestimated the man's natural laziness and under-guessed his shrewdness and friendship for Krimble.

"A promise," Anse said. "Lone Star shoots Sam Andrews from cover. Krimble denies it was even Lone Star that did it. He comes into my yard and says he's there to talk peace. Before Bovee died he admitted Krimble had given him orders to shoot me down.

"Krimble's promises. He sits up there like a brass-riveted king. He's got us beaten down until we talk farming." Anse held out his hands. "These won't fit a plough. Maybe Geldien's will. We all made a good living here once. The hills will be green again, but if we plough up our valley now, the only cows we'll ever run down here again will be milk cows. Krimble will be sitting up there laughing to himself.

80

"Every morning, Geldien, you can look at your wonderful wheat field, and wonder how long Krimble will let you have water. You'll live with that year in and year out—if it lasts that long. Then, one day, Krimble will throw a little dam across Calumet Creek and dig a little ditch, high up. Calumet will be running into Lost Creek and you won't have a drop of water.

"You can walk around then, Geldien, looking at the sky and whining, 'But he promised me!' Maybe it will rain then, and maybe it won't."

Anse shook his head. "Nairn is raising hay. We can all raise hay. Who'll buy it? Krimble—for nothing. The man wants not only what he's got, but he'll take everything down here too. What about it, Geldien? Latham?"

"This," Geldien said. He got on his horse. Latham mounted and they rode away.

"Damned good riddance," Big George growled. "When do we start the drive, Anse?"

"We won't have any trouble gathering cattle," Anse said. "Day after tomorrow we'll put 'em into the Lost Creek meadows and come home."

Odom scrubbed his buck teeth with his tongue. "And leave our stuff up there unprotected?"

Anse pointed down the valley, hard-cropped to the sod. "You're wishing you didn't have to see those cows on that until spring roundup, aren't you?"

Limberis and Big George laughed.

"They're going to stray, Odom," Anse said.

"Suppose Krimble starts shooting 'em?" Odom asked.

"You know he won't," Anse said. He smiled. "We'll get the sheriff after him if he does." His face hardened quickly. "Are you with us or not, Odom?"

"Yeah, yeah!" Odom said. "What else can a man do?"

81

When the Honeywells were riding alone down the valley, Barr spoke suddenly. "Geldien is right, Anse."

Too much talking to the women, his mother and Bitsy Miller; that, and the fact that Barr could not extend his thinking more than a mile from where he was born. "You think so?" Anse said.

"Yeah." Barr's mind was made up. Anse knew just how it worked. "I'll help with this drive day after tomorrow, but that's all."

"What will you do then, Barr?"

"I'm putting crops on my half of Seven Cross. You've got big plans, Anse, and they're too big for my stomach."

"I see." He did not need Barr or Seven Cross but at the moment he did need solidarity. Wavell's wedge was bad enough. It would not do to have Anse Honeywell's own brother back out now.

"I see," Anse said, and he was seeing much farther than Barr could imagine. He could not bully Barr, he knew; you got around him but you could not drive him when his mind took one of its stubborn sets.

They jogged along in silence among Odom's lankribbed cattle.

After a long time Anse spoke in a tone of brotherly interest. "How is it with you and Bitsy?"

"It'll be better when she knows I'm getting shet of the cattle business. Her old man like to have starved to death trying to raise cows. She hates 'em."

"I see your point," Anse said. "Of course right now we need every man. You stick in this scrap until we lick Krimble and I'll give you my half of Seven Cross."

Barr thought it over, scowling. At last he said, "No. I'm getting out after I help with the first drive."

It was just the answer Anse had expected, and so it

82

seemed to justify what he must do now. "There's just one thing, Barr—I don't want you to blow up when I tell you—but I wish you'd pick another girl besides Bitsy. I'll go along with you no matter what you decide, you understand, but I do wish you'd pick somebody besides that girl."

Barr stopped his horse. "What do you mean?"

"Ma doesn't know, I'm damned sure, or she wouldn't have Bitsy around the place. I've never mentioned what I know to anyone, so maybe the thing is sort of forgotten by now. From the bottom of my heart, I hope so."

"What do you mean!"

"You recall when Bitsy first left her folks, when her old man pulled out for Oregon or Montana? Bitsy was pretty young when she went to stay with Dutch Holcomb. I hold Wavell more responsible for it than Bitsy. You know how smooth-tongued he is, and him being the sheriff and all—"

"Damn you, Anse! What are you trying to say?"

"You remember he was always dancing with her there in Dutch's, sort of herding the over-anxious boys away. Well, he wasn't doing it for nothing, Barr. I happened to go to his office late one night . . . Ma doesn't know, Barr, so there's no need to tell her."

"You're lying, Anse!"

Anse sighed. He shook his head. "I wish now I'd kept still about it, but you're my brother and I don't like to see you take on something second-hand. Wavell . . . old enough to be her father. No, I'm not lying, Barr."

The bony structure of Barr's face was pushing hard against the skin. He looked sick and gray.

"I say I wish you'd turn to someone else, maybe one of Shepherd's oldest girls, Barr, but that depends on how much you're gone on Bitsy. It was a long time ago, and you couldn't blame her too much, just fresh away from her folks and—"

"I can blame Wavell!" Barr almost choked. The pits of rage were popping now, and his mind was channeled in one of its straight, hard lines.

"For God's sake, don't tell Ma. She's got enough worry now, thinking we're headed up the devil's road," Anse said.

Barr grabbed the cheek strap of Anse's bridle when Anse started to ride on, pulling the horse around so that the stirrups of the two men were touching. Barr's right arm and shoulder were trembling and his fist was cocked.

"You're sure, Anse? This ain't another of your dirty lies?"

Steadily Anse faced his brother's blazing look. "I'm sorry, Barr. I wish now I'd kept my mouth shut. You know there's always a chance I could have been wrong."

"Don't try to change it now! You said you saw them!"

"Well, I . . ." Anse shook his head gently. "She was young, Barr, and that Wavell—"

"That's enough!" Barr let go of the bridle and swung his horse away. He was silent the rest of the way to Seven Cross.

At supper Amanda Honeywell asked sharply, "What's keeping Barr?"

"He's in the bunkhouse, staring at the ceiling," Anse said. "He doesn't feel like eating."

Mrs. Honeywell looked from Anse to Jeff and back again, and there was no difference in her expression. She waited until Jeff had gone. "The other day when me

84

and Bitsy talked to Barr, the day that man—" she nodded toward the doorway through which Jeff had just passed "—murdered Bovee, Barr was of a mind to do what his Pa always talked of, raising crops. You ain't tried to change his mind, have you, Anse?"

"No, Ma." Murder. She kept throwing the word at him, as if he had shot Bovee himself.

"You're lying, Anse. What did you do to Barr?"

Because she could anger him at all there was more anger against himself, fragmenting purpose. Anse headed for the door, but he could not leave without striking back.

"Maybe Barr found out that your precious Bitsy girl once planted her crops without building her fences first."

"That's fouler than the devil's heart! That's a dirty lie, Anse Honeywell!" Mrs. Honeywell went past Anse and ran toward the bunkhouse.

A mistake, anger, always a mistake, Anse thought; but she would not get anything out of Barr, not the way he was at the moment.

Jeff was standing at the corner of the corral, looking at the mountains. Anse went over to him. "We'll gather a hundred head tomorrow, Arbuckle." Anse pointed. "Along with nine hundred more, they're going up there."

Jeff nodded. Looking at the stony face, Anse found it impossible to believe Barr's story about the old man being utterly out of his head that day in the hayloft.

Together they looked at the mountains, and through the dusk the murmur of Amanda Honeywell's voice in the bunkhouse became slower and more hopeless as she tried to talk to a son who would not answer.

Vanita and Clay, heading for Lone Star, left the gray

85

hills. The mountains came flowing down to meet them, bearing gifts of living grass and trees and clear water. Behind them, the hills spread wide in sullenness, abandoned ant mounds threaded by streams that ran to a common joining on the edge of flatness.

"They thought there would be grass down there forever," Vanita said. "Look at it now."

They followed a trail in a deep valley where the aspens were as thick as a man's body, blackened at the boles from lack of sunlight. The odors of forest death were strong, but from the decay new life was rising. Clay felt better when they lifted from the gloom and reached sunny parks where fish were ringing the surface of beaver ponds.

"Don't ever shoot a beaver," Vanita said. "My father would string you up by your thumbs."

"What made you think I would?"

"You practice with your pistol, don't you?"

"Not on beavers." The conversation lingered in Clay's mind, troubling him.

Star-branded cattle along the creeks were fat and spooky, crashing toward the trees at the first glimpse of the riders. This range was not ridden frequently, Clay thought. With fifteen men at Star and twenty miles of mountains . . . There were probably four-year-olds that had never seen a man or horse at close range.

"How many men do you have on roundup?" Clay asked.

"About seventy. I wish we had 'em now."

One thousand cattle missed on roundup, or even two thousand, meant little. The grass was here to hold them and the cover to protect them and if the natural losses from cold and wolves and other causes ran five times higher than normal on an open range, there would still be calves beyond counting. It was a simple economy of plentitude that made Clay blink, for on the long trails behind him he had seen the cattle empires vanishing, by wire, by their own weight.

Star's domain was something to clutch at a man's thoughts and make him wonder.

They stopped on a bench and Clay drank in the vision of a land that was utterly different when looked at from the hills below. From down there it was only greenness; from here it was timber, parks, grassy ridges and the endless gleam of beaver-stored water. He could grasp now the meaning of empire.

He remembered, too, what Wavell had said about making instead of having or getting; and he wondered how Krimble thought he had made this. Keeping it the way it was did not mean building, necessarily.

Vanita was watching him. "You like it, don't you? I love it too."

There was no need to say more, Clay thought, but she went on. "There's more than thirty brands down in the hills. What would happen if they were all turned loose up here?"

Clay thought about it: men looking sidewise at each other's spreads, tallying mentally, throwing more cows on the range all the time. They would strip the mountains of their lushness, and then they would blame each other.

"How much of this does your father own?"

"He owns the water, and a half dozen small outfits that used to be here. The rest is his by right of use."

"What happened to the half dozen small outfits?"

"Bought out. Run out." Vanita made no bones about it. "They would have crowded each other, in time, and ruined everything. There's room for one brand here."

That was old and familiar; whether it was right or wrong Clay did not know. "You're an only child?"

"Yes.

Their horses crunched grass while they sat there looking at each other, both understanding much.

"If he won't do everything possible to protect this, I will," Vanita said. "I'll be here alone someday, until I get married of course."

Her words were man-like, her expression was direct and clear, but lying behind the words was a promise and a future. "This will all be mine someday, Clay," she said softly.

He was a drifter, a pistolman, one who had lately shed loneliness by the simple act of gaining two friends. Billy Nairn had offered him a hay ranch, and that had seemed to be everything Clay wanted.

Surely he was wrong, reading something into Vanita's eyes because he lacked experience. She wanted help for her father, that was all. There was no invitation or promise beyond her words. One half of him was still the shy, open-mouthed kid of the wheat valley, and he was dreaming.

Looking at her, bringing to hard concentration his methods of gauging men, he knew he was trying to think away a fact: the promise was there. Direct as she was, if she had wanted less from him, she would have asked less and promised nothing.

"It's not all just a matter of saving Lone Star for now or later. No, Clay; that isn't all of it."

A soft warmth was on her face now and he could no longer apply his reading skill. That was the way a woman looked at a man, he thought. There was a hotness and a pounding in his blood that beat the drums of wanting. The tension lines fell away around his mouth. His breath would not go all the way down.

He was looking at a woman now and not a problem.

She smiled at him and said, "You are not at all a cold man, Clay Arbuckle." She sent her horse on up the trail.

He followed, cursing a shyness that had left him gaping when he should have acted.

Lone Star was situated just short of heavy timber at the upper end of a huge mountain meadow. The buildings were rooted to the land by being products of the land, foundation stones of reddish rock, yellow pine logs two feet in diameter, overlapping the corners of the ranch-house by six feet.

All roofs were of shakes. They must have been split three feet long and an inch thick, Clay thought, and now they gleamed with white paint. In the middle of the yard was the emblem, a gigantic star outlined with peeled logs and set up on a tower of red sandstone. A lantern arm ran between two points of the star.

Krimble must be from Texas, sure enough, Clay thought, for Texans always tried to carry part of the state with them, never forgetting where they were from and never allowing anyone else to forget either.

From a barn large enough to hold fifty horses came a man, walking slightly bent. It was Art Kelley, the cowboy the Honeywells had beaten the day Clay first saw Sash. He recognized Clay, and there was no friendliness in the look.

"Is my father home yet, Art?" Vanita asked.

"In the house." Kelley followed the riders across the yard to where they dismounted before a gate in a low sandstone wall. A wide graveled walk, running between flower gardens, went up to the deep porch of the house, which faced south.

"All ranchhouses should face south," Jeff always

89

said. "Show me one that don't and there's a fool inside it." Clay wondered why he had thought of Jeff at this moment; for weeks his thinking had been free of his father's arbitrary statements. Maybe it was because he was nervous and unsure, coming here where he was not wanted, his presence dependent on a woman.

For the first time in his life he was conscious of setting his facial muscles to cover his thoughts. Shyness, or the ice-blooded heritage of his father? He wished he had not come.

Jim Krimble was striding down the graveled walk, crunching his boots hard, walking like a man with an unpleasant task to settle quickly. Clay glanced at Kelley. The cowboy had picked up the reins of the two horses, but he was waiting.

"Dad, I want you to meet—"

"He doesn't belong here, Nita."

"Since when are my friends unwelcome at Lone Star, Jim Krimble?"

Vanita's odd use of her father's name lanced through Clay's embarrassment; and then he was making anger against Krimble, building resentment of the man's arrogance. They prodded each other with their eyes, two dark-browed men letting their dislike of each other crackle in the air between them.

"I don't want him around," Krimble said.

"Your manners are bad," Vanita said.

Clay was no longer dependent on a woman. His pride was urging him to turn away unhurriedly, without words, to ride slowly past the emblem in the yard, and let his whole demeanor say to hell with Lone Star. That was his pride, but under it the coyote cries were sounding in his ears, their chorus springing quickly from Krimble's rebuff.

So he held his face tight across his feelings, ready to leave.

From the porch a woman called, "That's no place to visit, Jim. Vanita, bring the young man inside."

It was something like the breaking of a man's courage just short of drawing his pistol; somewhat like that but with a difference: it was belligerence, not courage, that ran out of Krimble.

Kelley was leading the horses away. He had started immediately after the woman called.

Going up the walk, Vanita held to Clay's arm. Krimble walked on the other side. "Remember, Nita," he said, "your mother doesn't know who killed Bovee." Krimble threw his hostility at Clay with one more glance, but by the time they reached the porch, the rancher's features had smoothed out.

Vanita at thirty-five, Clay thought. This slender woman whose blue-checked gingham skirt fell full to the porch had the same high cheek bones, the same blonde hair, the same cleanly molded features; but there was a gentleness in her expression, perhaps from maturity, a gentleness that was very nearly sadness.

"My mother, Mr. Arbuckle," Vanita said.

With his hat in his hands Clay bowed slightly.

"Vanita has spoken of you, Mr. Arbuckle, and now we are glad to welcome you here." Mrs. Krimble looked at her husband. "You remember her mentioning him, don't you, Jim?" There was a vagueness on the surface of her words.

"I remember," Krimble said.

"Oh?" Still looking at her husband, Mrs. Krimble smiled. That gentle glance, Clay suspected, saw just about as much as Vanita's sharper scrutiny.

"If my husband appears a trifle moody, you will have

91

to forgive him, Mr. Arbuckle. He's been greatly worried about trouble with the hill ranchers. It will all work out, I'm sure. Did you notice the flowers as you came up the walk? The phlox is unusually beautiful this year."

Clay looked at the garden. "Phlox is my favorite mountain flower."

"Oh?" Mrs. Krimble said politely. "Which is the phlox, Mr. Arbuckle?"

"The tall blue ones."

Mrs. Krimble smiled. "Won't you come in, Mr. Arbuckle?"

Clay saw that Krimble was squirming inside, and he saw Vanita give her father a casual what-did-I-tell-you glance.

The room Clay entered was beamed with polished red cedar. The walls were panelled with cypress. There was an impression of fragility about the furniture that made him want to tiptoe.

He put his hat on a rack near the door, and he hung his pistol belt there also. The latter seemed out of place on the rack, so he folded the belt around the holster quickly and laid it on the floor behind the base of the rack. Krimble's satiny black eyes were watching.

"Tell Margaret we'll have a guest for dinner, Vanita," Mrs. Krimble said. "Perhaps Mr. Arbuckle would like to refresh himself. Show him where."

Vanita took Clay's arm. As they passed the doorway of the dining room a golden caster on the table caught Clay's eye. Something seemed to leap at him. He stopped abruptly, staring through the doorway.

"What is it, Mr. Arbuckle?" Mrs. Krimble asked. "Is something wrong?" She started to cross the room.

"That—that thing on the table there . . ." Whatever it was that had startled Clay was gone now. "It's beautiful," he said.

"Yes," Mrs. Krimble said in a slow voice. "Thank you."

Before Vanita left Clay she patted his arm lightly. "My father," she said. "He has no call to be grumpy about your being here. He falls all over Fluffy Ruffles when she comes around."

"Fluffy Ruffles?"

"Bitsy Miller."

Ten men rode into the yard while women were putting food on the table in the big dining room. "I do hope there's been no trouble," Mrs. Krimble said.

Krimble went outside. Clay saw him talking to old Chauncey Wade, who pointed south and moved his long arms in expressive gestures. The riders put their horses away, and Wade came in with Krimble.

"Uh-huh, I know him, Alice," Wade said when Mrs. Krimble started to introduce Clay.

"There was no trouble, Chaunce?" Mrs. Krimble asked.

"No. Not this time," her husband said.

"There shouldn't be any. It will all pass."

Mrs. Krimble was not exactly vague; maybe she just had a lot of faith, Clay thought, but she sure didn't know what she was talking about. Maybe she had tempered her husband down a great deal, she and Ben Wavell, but it wasn't going to last forever. Clay was too sure of the explosive force in Jim Krimble.

From Jeff Clay had learned one habit which gave him no regret now: eating manners. Even in camp Jeff had been persnickety about how a man handled his grub.

"We pushed 'em back toward the hills," Wade said. "There'll be a lot drift back but we did the best we could." Wade was across the table from Clay, with

93

Vanita on one side of Clay and Krimble on the other. When Wade talked it was sometimes difficult for Clay to tell whether the foreman was speaking to him or Krimble.

"They'll come again, somewhere else," Krimble said.

"Perhaps not, Jim," his wife said.

"You know they will, Mother!" Vanita looked at Clay. "Won't they?"

"I don't know. I stick close to Sash myself."

After an awkward pause Krimble said, "Tell Nairn he can have a couple of hay racks. You can take one down tonight, if you want to." He seemed to doubt Clay's ability to handle a team. "What he really needs down there is a bailer."

"What he needs is about six fighting men," Vanita said. "Once the Honeywells see his hay headed up here—"

"Vanita, let's have no bunkhouse talk at the table." Mrs. Krimble was unruffled. She managed to press a firmness down on every outbreak of the undercurrent of thought that pervaded the table. "Anse Honeywell, for all his hungry appearance, has always acted like a gentleman. And Barr—well, he and Bitsy are planning to be married, and there isn't a finer girl than Bitsy."

It was a very good time to keep silent, Clay thought. The others seemed to think so too.

Sometime later Clay saw Chauncey Wade watching him with a dead-still expression. Clay was spinning the caster with the tip of his finger, watching the light flash on the ornate gold markings of the cruets.

"That's one nice thing about being a guest," Vanita said. "I used to get my hands smacked for that."

Surprised, feeling silly, Clay withdrew his hand. Mrs. Krimble was watching him sharply. "Sorry, ma'am. I

94

just—I don't know why—"

"Why, that's quite all right, Mr. Arbuckle." Mrs. Krimble smiled. "Vanita has always been utterly fascinated by that caster. I've always considered it a horrid piece, but—Twirl it all you wish."

Clay picked up his fork, cursing the impulse that had made him do a childish act. The moment passed. Krimble had not noticed. He was deep in his own thoughts. Mrs. Krimble began to talk about her flowers. Vanita gave the caster a hard spin, and then winked at Clay.

Wade was still staring at his plate, his lips pushed out, the bones of his face jutting hard. In a moment he began to eat again.

After the meal Mrs. Krimble would have directed a leisurely session over her coffee in the living room, except that no one but herself was in the mood. Clay was uneasy, wanting to leave, still thinking of how he had made a fool of himself at the table.

Wade excused himself at once, saying he would see about a team and hay rack, if Clay cared to handle a pair of spooky horses that had not been worked much lately.

Clay thought it over. Nairn had mentioned once that they might be able to borrow a hay rack from Krimble.

Nairn was independent; perhaps he had not wanted to ask. "I'll take it," Clay said. He thanked Mrs. Krimble for the meal. He was still talking when his eyes strayed to the dining room, where two women were clearing the table. The caster . . . he guessed he had been caught by it because he had never seen one made of gold before.

He almost forgot his pistol. Krimble did not; he handed it to Clay without comment. On the porch Krimble lit a cigar, looking at Vanita and Clay. "I could be all wrong about you, Arbuckle, but I don't think I am. Until I know more, don't you come here on visits any more."

Vanita said, "Dad! You know he—"

"Be quiet, Vanita. You heard me."

His wife might twist Krimble around her finger, Clay thought, but Vanita could not do it. In spite of the man's bluntness Clay felt a touch of understanding. Krimble was under heavy pressure. His worries must be bad enough, with having his natural fighting tendencies restrained by a woman. Krimble must love his wife a whole lot.

Clay watched the Lone Star owner stride away toward the bunkhouse. No matter how much Krimble loved his wife, there must be times like this when he was glad to get out of the house.

"I'll change his mind about you, Clay," Vanita said. "Now that you've been here, what do you think of Lone Star?"

"Quite a place."

"You wouldn't want to see it wrecked, would you?"

"No."

"It's simple, Clay. Stop the Honeywells and there will be no trouble."

Clay looked away from Krimble's back and studied Vanita. It was there once more, the invitation and the promise. Bitsy had warned him about being talked into something.

Looking at Vanita, Clay found it easy to justify her attitude, and easier yet to believe everything her words and look implied.

"It's so simple, Clay," she said.

She made it seem so, but moments later, walking across the yard alone, Clay knew it was not simple at all because he did not know his own mind. He would have to talk to Wavell about all this.

Standing beside the hay rack, Chauncey Wade pointed. "That's the road, Arbuckle. You can't get off it until you reach the hills. Where you from?"

"A little place in Kentucky." That was what Jeff had said. Clay's horse was tied behind the rack. Kelley handed up the lines to the heavy team and went back inside the barn.

"Where in Kentucky, Arbuckle?"

"I forgot."

"That's your father at Seven Cross, ain't it?"

Clay nodded.

"I don't generally poke so hard unless I like a man," Wade said. "I like you well enough to say I think you ought to move right on out of the country."

"I had nothing to do with Bovee." Clay drove away.

Bleak and puzzled, Wade watched the rack jounce across the creek. The team was full of fire but Clay was handling them. Wade was still watching when Vanita told him her mother wanted to see him.

"In a minute." Chauncey Wade wondered where he would be today and what kind of man he would be if he had settled down with a family of his own, instead of tying his destiny to a friend who was always having trouble with his women.

Alice Krimble was waiting beside a massive desk in the little room where her husband kept accounts. "Close the door, please, and sit down."

Wade closed the door but he did not sit down.

"Chaunce, what about that boy tonight?"

"He's no boy. What about him?"

Mrs. Krimble kept looking at him until Wade knew he was in for a bad session this time.

"You saw what I saw, Chaunce."

"Saw what, Alice?"

"For one, the caster. Most casters don't spin at all, but that boy reached out knowing that he could make it turn. He was absolutely puzzled, away from us all, and—"

"Lots of casters spin."

"Not the way that hideous piece does. It's the only possession of that woman's I have in the house. Even if Jim has forgotten, you yourself have told me—"

"Jim don't know. Maybe I made that story up, when you kept asking me what the boy was like. It's been so long—"

"So long ago that Clay Arbuckle didn't even realize why he was attracted to that horrible thing. I tell you, Chaunce, the way he stared and reached out with his hand—and Jim didn't even notice. If he hadn't been so involved in worrying about a few stray cattle on his land. . ."

"There is a little resemblance, yes, but—" Wade shook his head. "I was worrying about something else. I just happened to be staring across the table, that's all."

"Indeed you were, Chauncey Wade. There were little gestures, and something in the eyes, and once the boy smiled at me. Jim used to smile, before he got at odds with the Honeywells. You saw that smile, and you almost dropped the food off your fork, and then you kept looking from one of them to the other and I saw the truth of your thoughts, even if you won't admit them now.

"He is the boy, Chaunce. He's the one lost after that stampede. You know he's Jim's son, and I do too."

Wade shook his head, not too emphatically. "His father is at Seven Cross, Alice."

"Have you seen him?"

"Well, no, not exactly."

"Bring that man to me, Chaunce. I want to talk to him."

"Good God! Pardon me, Alice. I mean, that can't be done. He works for Anse Honeywell. He's the one—I can't bring him here."

"And why not?"

"I just told you!"

"Then I'll go talk to him. Have Kelley get a rig ready to drive me to Seven Cross tonight, at once."

"Arbuckle isn't there now. He's been scouting the mountains for the hill men. There's no telling when he'll be there."

"Then I'll have Jim send someone to find this Arbuckle, wherever he is."

"Great Jesus! Pardon me, Alice. We can't do that. Don't you understand?" Wade grabbed at anything that would help her admit understanding. "He's the one that killed Bovee. It wasn't no accident, like we said. Jeff Arbuckle, Clay's father, killed Bovee in cold blood."

Mrs. Krimble turned pale. "Texas all over again," she murmured. "Will it never cease." A few moments later she rallied strongly. "That gives us proof that the man is not Clay's father."

Wade was dazed, just when he thought he was coming clear. "Proof? How the—How do you figure?"

"Clay Arbuckle is a gentleman, Chaunce, no matter how frozen and wary he looks at times. He is not the kind who would kill a man. Like father, like son. Therefore, this man at Seven Cross is not his father. Of course, we both admit that—"

"Not me. I don't admit it." Wade was confused by her devious reasoning.

"We both admit the man is not his father, but now the evidence is positive. Perhaps I won't even have to talk

99

to the man now. I'll talk to Jim instead."

"No," Wade said desperately. "He's got trouble enough. Let's be sure before we say anything to Jim."

"Very well. Bring me this Jeff Arbuckle then."

"You're too sure, Alice. It ain't him."

Mrs. Krimble shook her head slowly. "You and Jim and Vanita can mislead me in matters where I choose to be misled, but this is different."

"We're not sure."

She looked at him for a long time, smiling faintly. He wondered if he had ever fooled her in any matter.

"You and I are sure," she said. "Aren't we, Chaunce?"

Wade said nothing.

"And you'll get the man for me at once?"

"It won't be like that. It'll take some doing."

After a moment Mrs. Krimble said, "Ah, yes, I suppose it will take a little time. But I trust you, Chaunce, except when I know and accept the fact that you're misleading me about violence, such as Jack Bovee's death." She let out a long breath. "It really is a desperate time for Lone Star, isn't it?"

Wade nodded. They looked at each other starkly.

The sadness ran across her face again and she withdrew from unpleasant fact once more. "I'm sure it can be settled without more bloodshed," she said. "Get the man for me."

"It might be in South Fork."

"That will be satisfactory. I must see Mrs. Archer about some millinery soon, so that will be all right."

Wade thought his mind was sharp enough as soon as he was out of the room. His tongue had got away from him. He had contradicted himself, talked like an idiot.

He watched Vanita go into the kitchen, and he heard

her give an order to one of the women washing dishes. She had been in the hall when he came out. Just passing the door, or listening?

He went out on the porch and stood there with his hat in his hands, watching the light fading on the slopes that protected the valley.

That boy . . . He is a gentleman . . . A pistolman if ever Wade had seen one. He was Kevin Krimble, all right. It hit you right between the eyes when you looked at the two of them together.

Down there on the Big Red that night the stampede had run till morning, with two men dead and both Krimble and Wade thrown from their horses in the darkness. It was still raining when they walked back to the camp. The cook was there, smashed into the mud under the wreckage of his wagon. A dying steer was kicking him in the chest every time it moved spasmodically.

But Kevin was gone. There was nothing but mud and the rain and the river slobbering over its banks. They searched the plain, much farther than the distance a boy could have run in the little time he would have had to run; and then they went downriver and that was hopeless too.

Jim Krimble did not speak altogether from the fever and the pain when he said, "Maybe it's best, Chaunce. It wipes out all that part of my life."

Wade walked slowly off the porch and was in the yard before he remembered that this was not his decision at all; he had made a promise to Alice Krimble. The only way Wade wanted to see Jeff Arbuckle was dead, dead for his cold-blooded shooting of Bovee.

But there was the promise. Wade wondered how he got so tangled up.

Barr Honeywell stayed in the timber most of the way on his return from scouting the actions of Lone Star at Big Spruce hogback. He was still in the fight because nothing seemed to matter much, not after Anse's revelation about Bitsy and Ben Wavell. Every time Barr tried to think of pulling out to raise crops on Seven Cross, Wavell stood between him and the other half of the dream.

Second hand . . . It depends on how much you're gone on her, Barr . . .

For days corrosive thinking had been eating into Barr. When he woke in the morning his thoughts snapped right back to where they had left off the night before. Bitsy and Wavell. It might have been different if Wavell had wanted to marry her, but the way it stood it was a matter of a smooth-tongued, filthy old cuss taking advantage of a scared kid.

And the kid was Bitsy, and Barr had wanted to marry her.

Where the aspen slopes broke down to the first gray hills, Barr saw a rider coming up the road. Something twisted hard inside him. He knew the horse, and after awhile the set of the rider in the saddle was familiar too.

Wavell! Wavell! The thought was like a scream.

Barr's hands were trembling when he tied his horse to an aspen. He pulled his rifle from the scabbard and rested it across a limb. He waited. The light was getting poor, and Wavell, as usual, was not pushing his horse.

It was a long time, a matter of two minutes or more, but the interval closed. Barr took a deep breath. The .44-40 sent its sound in a long gush across the hills.

Below, the horse threw up its head and stopped. The rider moved slightly, bending forward a little, reaching

102

for the horn, and then he rolled sidewise out of the saddle.

Barr kept looking down the rifle barrel, with smoke drifting back into his face. Finally, when his lungs could no longer hold used air, his breath came out with a heave. For a time, everything that had ridden him through the days and nights was gone. Below, the horse drifted away from the man in the road and began to search for grass.

Wavell's eyes were open when Barr looked down at him. They were open and they blinked and they seemed to recognize Barr.

"That pays off for Bitsy!" Those were the words Barr had dreamed of saying, explosively, triumphantly; but now they were merely words, without much meaning.

Wavell's lips moved slowly. His eyes were puzzled. He made no sound and soon the eyes drifted away toward blankness, but his lips still moved a little.

Mixed with rage a terrible fear gripped Barr. "Did you hear me!" he shouted.

Wavell's slack mouth said, "Wrong . . . Barr . . ."

Wrong? About what? Bitsy, or this act? All at once everything was wrong, and Barr was standing again at a tree with his rifle across a limb. *O God! What made me pull that trigger!*

The gray face there in the dust was no longer the symbol of Barr's hatred. It was Ben Wavell, a man who had stood between Ma Honeywell with her two half grown kids and the greed of hill ranchers when they wanted to take over Seven Cross after the death of Barr's father. Ben Wavell had given Barr his first rifle.

Ben Wavell was dying now. Barr caught the sheriff's horse. He stripped the saddle from it. He put the saddle under Wavell's head, and spread the blanket so that it covered the small stain on Wavell's chest. The sheriff tried to speak again, but it was a formless whisper. He lay blinking his eyes tiredly.

Like a slicing wind fear drove into Barr. He ran to his horse and rode away. For a while the road he followed was truly the devil's road of his childhood dreams, and then all fear was natural, and so he set about covering up his trail.

There was a light in the house when he reached Seven Cross. He quieted the dogs when they came to meet him. Skirting the yard, he led his horse to the corral and took care of it, and then he stood there looking at darkness. He could not see the land where he had once thought he would raise crops. All he could see was Ben Wavell's face, the gray set upon it, and the dust in the sandy hair, and the hat lying to one side.

Dust.

Bitsy.

Turn back time two hours. Just two hours, God!

Mrs. Honeywell came out on the porch and called. "Barr!"

Silence. The dogs trotted to her.

"Who came in?"

Barr did not answer.

She spoke then to the dogs. "I swear I heard somebody. You, Bull, what was you fools a-barking at?"

Barr Honeywell stared into darkness.

Just before dark Clay thought he heard the sounds of distant gunfire but he could not be sure because of the rattling of the hay rack. On the last long slant to the hills the team tried to run and he had his hands full for a while. "When we get off this," he thought, "they'll get a

104

bellyful of running."

He was still on a long grade when the horses lay back suddenly until their rumps were almost down. They tried to twist off the road and then they tried to bolt. He quieted them and got down, going to their heads and talking to soothe them.

"Clay," a voice said in a whisper.

Clay spun around with his gun in his hand. A few moments later he stumbled over Wavell. The sheriff said no more. In the darkness, with the team shifting nervously a few feet away, Clay's hands told him part of the story when he started to lift Wavell.

With his shirt Clay made a compress to bind into the crater in the sheriff's back, and then he got Wavell onto the hay rack and went toward Sash faster than he had intended to. Several times, although he knew his sense of direction would not fail him, he thought he had turned off on a branching road.

Under starlight he came over the last hill into the valley where Sash lay. Everything was dark down there.

He was sure he had stopped in the yard, and then he was turned around because there were no buildings looming through the darkness. A drift of smoke across his face and then the overpowering odor of charred wood all around told the tale.

Sash was burned to the ground.

Clay knelt beside Wavell and tried to get a word from him. The sheriff's cheeks were cold. He was barely breathing. The compress was still in place, soaked now.

Cramping the rack around, Clay nearly turned it over. He cursed loudly, and it was soon after that a voice called his name.

Billy Nairn was lying on his side, over toward the west hill. His voice was strong enough. "My left arm," he said. "It's busted. My hip is all smashed up. Big George done it with a rifle."

Clay went toward South Fork with two wounded men in a hay rack. He stopped in the field long enough to throw on three shocks of hay, bedding Nairn and Wavell as best he could.

Nairn talked steadily, largely to fight away the agony of grating bones. "There was only a half dozen, Callaway, Hayden, Limberis—and some others. They came in when the hands were helping me fix the mower, just before dark.

"I waited too long. I knew better, but Big George was grinning. He cleared his rifle, Clay, while I was trying to get my pistol."

The wagon jounced heavily. Nairn clamped down on a groan.

"Were the Honeywells along?" Clay asked.

"No. Neither of them. They ran the drifters straight down the valley, shooting over their heads. I was laying in front of the blacksmith shop. They run the spring wagon against it, and the mower too. They set fire to everything. My boots were on fire before I got up guts enough to crawl clear."

Nairn kept talking, until the jolting descent on Little Squaw hill knocked him into a state of semiconsciousness.

Clay pounded the door of the Horseshoe, and while he was waiting he tried to see across the street to the sheriff's office, remembering himself and a friendly, rosy-cheeked man who had talked to him over there.

Dutch Holcomb asked, "Who's there?"

Clay told him and said, "I want a doctor."

Dutch was lighting a lamp when Bitsy came running, throwing a wrapper around herself. "Who's hurt?"

106

Staring toward the gloomy wall where he had been sitting not long before, Clay thought: *I could have stopped them in their tracks that day. I could have killed about half of them.* He looked at Bitsy. "Wavell and Nairn."

"I'll get Doc Covert," Bitsy said.

She was back with him by the time Dutch and Clay had carried the injured men to poker tables under one of Dutch's brightest lights. Nairn was conscious.

Doc Covert was a husky, red-bearded man, much wrinkled from using all the muscles of his face to laugh. He examined Nairn quickly, scarcely glancing at the broken arm, working the shattered hip with what seemed to be brutal roughness to Clay.

"That's a nice mess. How'd you burn the soles off your boots, Billy?" the doctor asked.

Between gritted teeth Nairn said, "Fire, you damned fool. Am I crippled?"

"Not yet," Covert said cheerfully. "Put him on a bed. Bitsy—no feather mattress. See if you can get some of the dirt and shredded cloth out of that wound."

When Clay and Dutch returned from carrying Nairn to a room, Covert was putting a fresh compress on Wavell's back. "How long ago?" the doctor asked.

"Sometime before dark," Clay said.

"Did he cough up from the lungs?"

Clay shook his head.

Covert finished his work. The Rivers light above the table showed all the laugh wrinkles on his face but they were empty channels now and his expression was distant and contained. "I couldn't have helped much if I'd been there at the time," he said. "He'll die in a few hours."

Dutch looked at Clay, and then Dutch turned away.

107

"I'll get dressed, Arbuckle, and take care of the horses. A hay rack for Ben Wavell. That wasn't right."

The first feeling of bleak light was sliding over South Fork when Wavell died. Covert rose from his chair at the bed and reached for the blanket. Standing in the doorway of the room, Clay said, "Don't pull it up. He had nothing to hide his face from."

Covert went out and down the hall to a room where Bitsy was sitting beside Nairn.

Bleak and lonely as the pre-dawn coyote cries coming from the plain, Clay stood looking at the first friend he had ever known.

Bitsy touched his arm gently. "You'd better go to bed now, Clay."

You went all your life lonely and unhappy, killing men you did not want to kill, and then you found somebody who smiled and invited you into the warm circle of mankind. This happened then.

"Go to bed, Clay."

Start with Big George Callaway, and then the Honeywells. Keep right on going. Leave them with their faces strange and thin like Ben Wavell's.

In a long quaver, a savage chorus calling for blood, the coyote cries rolled off the plain.

Bitsy led him down the hall, past the room where Covert sat beside a big blond man whose face was pale and quiet now, whose burned feet were bulky lumps in bandages. Even without the hip damage, Clay doubted that Billy Nairn would ever walk again like other men— and raise the biggest hay crop there ever was.

"In here," Bitsy said. "Sleep is what you need."

Clay sat on the edge of the bed. His mind was a weary hub and thoughts from all directions rushed down the spokes to torment him. Ben Wavell sat in the stubble of a hayfield with a broken pipe stem in his teeth and made a wry remark, and Billy Nairn was laughing.

"Lie down and go to sleep." Bitsy was watching from the doorway.

Dutch Holcomb came down the hall, trying to walk quietly. He stood beside Bitsy. "I didn't notice Ben's rig was in that rack last night. How come?"

"The saddle and blanket was there with him," Clay said. "On the ground."

"On the ground?" Dutch frowned. "I wonder—"

"Leave him alone, Dutch," Bitsy said.

"I was just going to say that when I put the horses in Frost's barn last night, Billy Smithers woke up—he was sleeping in the hay. I didn't tell him nothing, but later on he found the saddle and blanket and now he's stirring the whole town up."

Bitsy took Dutch away. After a while Clay pushed the door shut and rolled over on the bed.

They came out of the darkness and the rain, bellowing their madness, with the fire dripping from their horns.

"You're all right. You're all right, Clay." The voice went on and on and it was soothing. It was Bertha's voice, so Clay clung hard to her until the terror was gone.

And then he was sitting up, still fully dressed, holding Bitsy Miller in his arms. It was broad daylight. She stood away from him then, looking at him with a troubled expression.

"Ben told me about that stampede. He seemed to know an awful lot about you, Clay. How often do you have those nightmares?"

"Not often." Clay was gruff. He heard the mutter of many voices in the saloon, and knew that his outcries must have reached there.

There was something more than sympathy in Bitsy's eyes, for sympathy can run quickly on the surface, but what Clay saw was understanding. He told her about the stampede and about the wheat valley and before he knew it he was deep into his roving life with Jeff—and then he stopped.

"The moment I saw you," she said, "I thought you were the loneliest man I had ever seen. Ben Wavell would have called it hound-dog—"

Someone knocked on the door and a voice strange to Clay said, "He's awake now, Bitsy."

"He's had no breakfast. Go away."

"We've been waiting—"

"Go away, Will!"

The man left.

"When you're lonely come to me," Bitsy said. "If you want to."

Clay weighed the words, but most of all he read her face, and he was glad then that he had not jumped to error. He caught a glimpse of the depth of a woman, deep and wise, where before he had been looking at a pretty face.

"That was Will Shertz at the door," Bitsy said. "He's chairman of the board of county commissioners. They want to make you sheriff."

To do just what Clay intended to do anyway. A sheriff's badge might make it easier. First, Big George Callaway . . .

"Ben wore his star inside," Bitsy said. "He never acted just because there was a symbol on his vest. He was a pistolman, Clay, probably as good as they come. I think he could have killed Anse Honeywell without getting hurt."

"I'm thinking of Callaway."

"I'm thinking of you. A badge can't change what goes on in your mind. You've started to make a break here, Clay. Don't throw it away now."

"Callaway shot Billy Nairn without giving him a chance." Callaway or someone with him probably had shot Wavell too, on the way to Sash.

"He should pay for that," Bitsy said. "But don't set yourself up as the executioner."

"I don't understand you, Bitsy."

"I understand you, and so did Ben. You're not a killer, Clay, no matter what you've done in self-defense. Don't start being one. If Callaway or any of the rest come to you—"

"They won't! You know it!"

"Please don't do it, for your own sake."

"With Ben dead and Nairn crippled, you stand there and tell me that!"

"Ben would tell you the same thing."

"Ben's dead. You can have him say anything that pleases you." All his life Clay had been under someone's rigid control, and now this handful of woman was telling him what was good for him. He was a pistolman and the mark was on him. For the first time in his life he had reason and desire to use his skill offensively.

He stared at Bitsy. She was standing against the wall with her hands behind her, and on her face was an expression he could not read. Why didn't he brush her out of the way and go on about his business?

"Your breakfast is waiting." She walked out of the room.

All he had to do now was walk into the barroom and tell Shertz and the others he would take their job. They wanted a mess cleaned up with pistol work and he was qualified to do the job. They would not ask or care about his personal interest in the matter.

He did not go into the barroom, not just then. He washed and went down the hall to the kitchen, where Bitsy served him breakfast. He expected her to argue some more, but she said nothing.

"When's the funeral?" he asked.

"This afternoon."

Ben Wavell, singing on the mower, singing as he rode out on a futile peace mission . . . maybe he had been singing when the bullet caught him.

"I think I'll take the job," Clay said.

Bitsy said nothing. She did not even look at him.

Will Shertz was fat, with worry on his sweating face. He glanced at Clay's pistol, and the others with him glanced at Clay's pistol. Billy Smithers' purplish nose shoved into the circle, between the shoulders of two of the commissioners.

"He can do it, Will," Smithers said. "He's the boy!"

Shertz evidently had rehearsed an opening, but now he glanced briefly at Clay's set face and said, "We need a sheriff, Arbuckle. We're offering you the job."

"To handle any way I see fit?" Clay asked.

Shertz nodded. His eyes dropped to Clay's pistol again. "It can be stopped," he said. "It hinges on a few men only, and they've already violated the law."

"Name them," Clay said.

Shertz licked his lips. He was a townsman, a businessman. He was cautious and afraid. "Well—" he did not want to speak openly here before a crowd.

Smithers said, "Callaway shot Billy Nairn. Like as not he murdered Ben too. Anse Honeywell is keeping all the trouble going."

112

"You stay out of this, Smithers," Shertz said. His eyes made a little nod to Clay.

"Then there's Barr Honeywell," Smithers said. "He's not smart, but he's about as bad as Anse."

Shertz's eyes said yes, Barr too.

Dutch Holcomb spoke up angrily. "Smithers, you lied to Ben Wavell and took a bottle of whiskey from Anse Honeywell to set a trap for Krimble and Chaunce Wade. You get to hell out of here and don't come back!"

Smithers began to whine. "I'm a drinking man, Dutch. That explains it. I'm a drinking man." He went to the bar to plead with Dutch.

"Any way you want to do it, Arbuckle." Shertz looked sidewise at the other commissioners, and they were in agreement.

"For how much?" Clay asked.

Shertz narrowed his eyes and pushed out his lips. "Well now, let's see. Ben got seventy-five a month. Of course, he was an experienced man. Until you prove yourself we'd have to go a little less. Say, sixty-five?"

"Ben got ninety a month," Clay said. "He told me." Clay had been brutally sick of the whole matter ever since Shertz let Billy Smithers speak for him.

"We'll give you eighty."

Clay shook his head. "You could give me the town and it wouldn't be enough, not the way you've put it. How many of you will come out to Sash and help me put up Billy Nairn's hay, and build him a new house?"

Shertz frowned. "I don't quite get you. That is not in our line at all, Arbuckle."

"I see it isn't." Clay shoved his way through the crowd and went outside.

He heard someone complain, "Damn it, Shertz! You tried to save a few dollars and lost him."

113

"It wasn't the money at all," Dutch said. "It was the way you went at it. Get out of here, Smithers! I told you once to beat it!"

"Maybe we should have let you talk, Holcomb," Shertz said angrily. "Your business will suffer just as much as any of the rest if this quarrel drags on."

"Quarrel! Three men dead and you say 'quarrel.' I'll give each one of you sixty-five a month to go out and bring in Callaway and the Honeywells. I'll pay it in advance right now! How about it, Will?"

Clay walked up the street, out of hearing.

He started out of South Fork the way he had come, towing his horse behind the hay rack. The supplies on the rack were charged to Nairn, at Shertz's store. Men watched in silence when Clay stopped in front of the sheriff's office to leave a saddle and blanket at the door.

Clay was not going to Wavell's funeral, for the Ben Wavell he had known would not be there either.

Dutch Holcomb stopped Clay in the middle of the street when the hay rack was moving again. Dutch's face was flushed, but his eyes looked up without flinching. "I had you wrong, Arbuckle. I don't mind saying that Bitsy helped change my mind. If you need any help out there fixing up Nairn's place, ask for it. I can send you anything you'll need—" he looked at silent listeners "—anything but men.

"Thanks," Clay said, too tight inside to realize the full extent of what was being offered.

"We'll take care of Nairn," Dutch said.

All the way to Sash Clay tried to understand how much he had been influenced by Bitsy Miller before he made up his own mind that she was right about the sheriff's job.

When Clay drove over the last hill he saw four men

114

standing near the black fragments of the house. He slid his pistol up and down in its holster and slowed the team to a steady walk going across the valley.

He knew Fred Geldien, who introduced him to Terry Latham and the Dean brothers, the latter squat heavy men with perpetual scowls.

Geldien asked, "How's Billy?"

"Fair. Wavell is dead."

"Ben! Good Lord!" Geldien looked at his three companions. "We knew about this, but we hadn't—"

"He was shot on the Lone Star road, the last grade coming down. I found him there last night. How'd you know about this?" Clay asked.

"One of my kids came back with Billy," Geldien said. "Just for the trip. You know kids. He'd just headed back when he saw the start of things from the hill yonder. He streaked home but I'd gone to Latham's by then. He had to ride way up there, so by the time we got the Dean boys rounded up and came over, it was pretty late. Ben Wavell dead. Damnation!"

Parley Dean said, "I reckon me and Orley will just mosey over there where you found Ben, Arbuckle." His voice was slow and halting and he kept scowling while he talked.

Terry Latham was a hatchet-faced man with a fighter's gleam in his eye. He reminded Clay of a young Chauncey Wade. "Ben was at Callaway's," Latham said. "He tried to talk 'em out of pushing that gather into the mountains, but nobody listened. He went from there toward Lone Star. From what I heard, no one followed him to cut him down. Ben was awful well liked, and them that didn't care for him was just a mite afraid of him. I can't figure why he was killed."

"How do you know what happened at Callaway's?"

Clay asked.

"Ora Shelton pulled away from the Honeywell bunch when he found out Callaway was coming here," Latham said. "The Deans talked to him not long afterward."

The Dean boys nodded somberly. They went across the scorched yard, got on their horses and trotted up the valley toward the Lone Star road.

Geldien said, "Ben was trying mighty hard to hold a peace. That's what got him. He wasn't killed because they knew he was going to tell Krimble about this new drive. Old Wade and Krimble know all about that, don't you worry." He looked at the supplies on the hay rack, and then he sized Clay up as if he had not judged him accurately before.

"I got seven kids," Geldien said, "and a good chance to get burned out myself." He glanced at the ruins. "What's the first thing, a new house?"

They talked over the details. Latham said they could have all the timber they needed from Krimble, if they asked in advance of cutting. Geldien said that he and Latham would go to their ranches and get tools.

"Let's go whole-hog on this thing," Latham said. "Let's get the hay in while we're at it. Krimble's got a good mower and a rake in one of his high meadows, Arbuckle. While you're asking for timber, you'd just as well borrow that mower and rake too. Nairn could have got 'em, I know, but he was too proud to ask."

They were putting it on Clay. He did not care much about going to Lone Star, but he guessed Krimble could not call the trip visiting. While he was at it he would go past the place where he had picked up Wavell.

He found the Deans there, leaning against the cut bank, scowling at each other. They said they had scouted around. Parley pointed. "A man was on that hill.

He got off his horse and stood by a tree. There was some little limbs busted, like as if he cleared out to take aim across a bigger limb. No shell.

"That's his boot track right there, mixed in with yours. Up the road a piece is where he run to catch Ben's horse. He let the horse go. Then he rode that way." Parley pointed in the direction of Seven Cross.

"Why would he take off Ben's saddle?" Orley asked.

Clay studied the tracks of the horse that had come off the hill. A heavy horse, out-gaited, the shoes neither new nor badly worn. He thought perhaps he could track that horse across anything, even a lava plain. He was sure it was not Jeff's horse, but a man could ride in any saddle, on any horse.

Doubt and worry ate at Clay as he thought of Jeff's unusual actions lately. If Clay tracked the horse to Seven Cross, say, and discovered evidence that his father had killed Wavell—what then would Clay do? He thought of Jack Bovee. Why would a man, hot-headed perhaps, but cool enough to be trusted by Krimble in a tight situation, make a try for his pistol when he was riding away, knowing he was covered by unseen rifles?

"You reckon you could track that horse?" Parley Dean asked.

"Yes, I think so." Clay did not look at the Deans. "Later on. Right now I'm going to Lone Star."

"The tracks won't get no fresher," Orley said.

In the forest stillness where the road was soggy from the flow of springs he met Chauncey Wade. The Lone Star foreman sat his horse like a stiff-backed cavalryman and waited for Clay to come up.

They nodded. Wade appeared a little older each time Clay saw him. Clay spoke the first thought that came to his mind. "Why did you tell me to leave, Wade?"

"I owe you something, me and Krimble, for that day in the Horseshoe. You made enemies that won't forget, no matter who wins or loses this war. You'll get dragged into it if you stay. I thought maybe an old man could give you some advice."

The whole effect was too vague to satisfy Clay, although he was unable to grasp specific defects instantly. He doubted that he would do any better with further questions. He spoke then of Wavell and Nairn.

Wade's eyes looked out fiercely from their mesh of wrinkles. His face was set and tough. "Wavell liked you awful well."

"I think he did."

"Well, then?"

Clay shook his head. "I'll make up my own mind."

"You can always ride away."

"That's the last thing I have in mind."

"How well I know that." Wade was staring at the wet ground, a man lost to the present for a while. He seemed to be bearing only half his attention when Clay explained his reasons for going to Lone Star.

"Cut your timber," Wade said. "We won't be using the rake and mower this year, so you can pick 'em up tomorrow afternoon at the home place. Ordinarily we could give you more help than that, but you know how things are."

"Will it be all right with Krimble?"

"I said it, didn't I?" Wade looked hard at Clay. "That thing on the table you spun the other night—did you ever see one like that before?"

"Not like that one."

"Say you were going to play roulette on it, for rock candy—which cruet would be the winner?"

"Vinegar." Clay wondered where the answer had

118

come from. "I don't know. I don't follow you at all, Wade."

"You said vinegar. Why?"

"It popped into my head. What's the gag?"

There must be something wrong with Wade, Clay thought; the old cuss had spells when his face grew tight as if he had a bad pain. He was that way now, staring at the wet ground.

"It was just a gag, that's right." Wade turned his horse and started back the way he had come.

"I didn't figure to cause you extra riding," Clay said. "If Krimble is home, I can—"

"No need. I was headed for Seven Cross, but I changed my mind."

Half formed thoughts nagged Clay. Wade's behavior now added to the whispering of his mind, a rustling of expressions without clear shape. He watched the old man out of sight, and then he rode back to Sash.

Anse Honeywell was facing the Dean boys. Jingo, Wavell's horse, bare-backed, was near the side of the yard.

The Deans were on the edge of trouble, but afraid to take the step. They stood a few paces apart and scowled at Anse, two bulldogs wanting to grip a wolf.

Anse turned away from them and watched Clay swing down. "Maybe you have cooler judgment than my friends here, Arbuckle," Honeywell said calmly.

Clay walked toward him slowly, holding nothing but the thought that Anse could be held responsible for most of the trouble. He might just as well kill the man now. His mind frozen in that channel, Clay stopped and waited. Before, the others had always made the first move. Let Anse Honeywell be like the others.

His silence and his attitude stating clearly his

intention, Clay waited.

"Well, for hell's sake," Anse said slowly. "You too, Arbuckle?" His voice was pleasant. His deep eyes saw everything Clay wanted him to see, and they showed no fear, only mild surprise. "I bring a man's horse in when I find it trotting across my land. I find that the owner has been killed.

"First, the Deans, and then you, Arbuckle. Have you got any judgment at all?"

The Deans waited on Clay, and Clay knew he could not make the first move. It occurred to him, also, that Anse Honeywell might be able to afford letting him make the first move. Boxed in, Anse was still in control of the situation because of his relaxed calm. Maybe he was gambling; if so, he was a gambler such as Clay had never seen.

Clay let his eyes flick to the Deans. It was a trick that he had seen, to prompt the other man by appearing to give him a fraction of advantage. Anse made no move.

"I thought as much of Ben Wavell as any man," Anse said. "Orley, you and Parl know how he helped my mother after Pa was taken. Barr and me never forgot that. I've had my differences with Nairn, but I tried to keep him from being burned out. Big George Callaway moved behind my back to get the job done."

"Yeah, yeah, I know," Orley Dean said. "What I'm thinking is that a horse rode away from Wavell and went straight toward Seven Cross."

Anse nodded. "Barr was out. He was scouting Krimble's men near Big Spruce, but he never shot Ben. He thought too much of Ben, and you know it!"

Orley stared at the ground. "Somebody shot him."

"Track the horse," Anse said. "Track it to where it went. Barr is my only brother, but I'll lift my hands and

120

stand aside if there's any evidence that he shot Ben."

"I intend to track the horse," Clay said.

Anse turned his back and walked away. At his horse he looked around. "I came here friendly. I still have no quarrel with anybody in the hills. My fight is up there." He waved at the mountains. When he was on his horse he asked, "How is Nairn?"

Clay did not answer. He could not make up his mind about Anse Honeywell, other than that the man was the coolest, most dangerous person he had ever known.

"I like your father very well, Arbuckle," Anse said, "but somewhere along the line he neglected to teach you manners." He rode away unhurriedly.

"I don't know," Parley said. "He gets my thinking all out of gait. I don't know . . ."

Orley said, "He was bluffing. I've seen him do it in a poker game. You never know what he's thinking. You really going to track that horse, Arbuckle?"

"After a while."

Clay helped the Deans clear the twisted cook stove and other wreckage away from the building site. They pulled the fireplace chimney over with a rope and horse and used the stones to start a foundation.

"Pretty soon it'll be getting late for tracking," Orley said. "The longer a track stands in this sun—"

"I'm going in a few minutes," Clay said. "When do Geldien and Latham figure on being back?"

"Sometime this evening." Orley straightened up and rubbed his blackened hands across the small of his back. "You might nigh killed Anse, didn't you?"

"I thought of it," Clay said. He was glad now that he had not. He wondered what Bitsy would think of him if she knew. Vanita would say he had missed a good chance, and that was the way Clay was inclined to view the matter himself ; but still he was glad there had been no pistol work.

For a half mile the tracks Clay followed went up a road that wound between the hills, toward Seven Cross. The man had stopped a great many times, sometimes turning his horse to face the way he had come. Several times he had surged to the side of the road. Clay found nothing to explain the reason for the man's erratic behavior. He wondered if the man had been drunk.

When the tracks left the road, turning away at a wide angle, they were no longer pointed toward Seven Cross. Trailing was slow work then, for some of the hills were rocky. The sun was gone and evening was a promise when Clay stopped beside a shallow stream.

Here the rider had gone into the water. There was no way to tell whether he had gone up or down on the gravelly bottom, and there was no time for hours of patient searching. It was certain that he would have emerged where many cattle had been churning in and out of the stream. Because Seven Cross was downstream, Clay went in that direction. Before long he passed three tributary creeks. The man could have ridden up any of them.

The trail was dead and Clay knew it. Spooky at first, charging his horse to the side of the road like a wild man, the rider had steadied later, using his knowledge of the country to hide his tracks.

It was not Jeff; Jeff would have been cold-blooded from the first.

Not far from Seven Cross, in a thicket of tall willows, Clay almost rode against his father. Jeff was on the ground, waiting beside his horse. The twist of his mouth and the sneer in his eyes said that he had seen Clay from a long way off and had picked a place where their trails would meet.

"The kind of game you're trying to trail could have killed you with a rock, the way you come a-blundering."

Jeff had not changed a bit; but Clay had changed. He resented the cold pattern of his father's features, as well as the rebuke. For a while Clay was looking at a stranger, and then the commanding pull of old ties and associations asserted its force to put uneasiness and the fear of making a mistake deep into Clay.

He was afraid of his father; that was it. He had always been afraid of Jeff.

"Who did you have in mind?" Jeff asked.

"Maybe your boss."

"No. He was helping with the cattle at Callaway's place. I was there, We stayed the night there."

"Barr, then?"

"He was in the right direction. Did you try Chaunce Wade?"

"Wade?" Clay frowned.

"Two times Wade talked war to Krimble, and two times Wavell talked Krimble into doing nothing about hill cattle driven on Lone Star range. They're losing up there, Clay. Wade knows it, even if Krimble won't admit it. Maybe Wade saw Wavell headed up there to talk more peace. He's a bitter man, that Chaunce Wade. His happy home is sliding out from under him."

"No. It wouldn't be Wade. How about Callaway?"

"What direction did your man come from?"

"Out of the mountains."

The little twist of Jeff's wide mouth was like a smile, but it was not patience and never had been: it was merely contempt for stupidity.

"Callaway was down there fixing up your nest," Jeff said. "He wasn't near the mountains, him or none of them with him. You're getting to be quite a farmer, Clay."

"Is it any of your business?"

"You're even hanging around Lone Star."

"It's none of your business, Jeff."

"You said that one day a long time ago when I came to get you from the people I had paid to keep you. You didn't say it afterward. Now you're all mixed up, Clay, trying to be a farmer, trying to make friends with Lone Star, a mess of snakes if ever there was one.

"I know you, Clay. There's a wild black streak of blood in you, the same as runs in me. You're a killer, boy. I've tried to keep you from it, and five times you got away on me. You're getting worse. Today you tried every way you could to jump Anse Honeywell. You say it ain't none of my business?

"I raised you from a sniveling whelp, Clay. I tried to teach you how—"

"You taught me to size up every man I saw as a target!"

"Only to keep you alive for the day when I'd have to tell you something about yourself. Your mother was no good, and you've got her dirt all over you, and then you've got my wild streak too. I've learned to control mine, but you haven't—not without me around. You tried to kill Anse, and now you'd like to go down and jump Barr, just because he happened to be in the mountains the day the sheriff was shot.

"You see what I mean, Clay? That streak in you is insanity, and the only chance you got to beat it is to stick with me. You go back to your stinking hay field and think about it."

Jeff swung up and rode away.

He left behind him a shaken, white-faced man, with

all his vague suspicions of himself now gathered into a great cold lump that resembled truth.

Wild and lonely the coyote cries flooded Clay's mind. He was lost once more on the sage plain, and the only one who could help him was Jeff. The long years of dependence on his father told him to ride quickly after Jeff, to admit that he was right.

And he might have followed his father then, but Bitsy told him he was not a killer, and Dutch Holcomb, redfaced, came into the street and said the same thing without saying it at all; and Ben Wavell accepted him as a man and a friend; and Billy Nairn said they could hunt together in the winter.

They spoke and smiled, through the slicing knives of Jeff's cold words. After a while Clay put his horse across the creek, through the willows, and rode in the dusk toward Sash. That was where he wanted to go, but his eyes were tortured and the coyotes told him of his lostness.

Riding through the dark yard of Seven Cross, Jeff heard the bumping of Mrs. Honeywell's rocker. When the tempo slowed, he knew she had recognized him. The fact that Ma Honeywell hated his guts sort of tickled Jeff.

She said, "You tell Barr to come here when you go to the bunkhouse, Mr. Arbuckle. If you please."

"Yes, ma'am."

"He's acting strange, that Barr. He hasn't—"

"Yes, ma'am?"

"Nothing!"

She was desperate to talk to somebody, Jeff knew. Clay would be that way, after he brooded a while, and then he would come running to find out more about himself. Jeff went to the corral and unsaddled.

When he entered the bunkhouse, Barr was lying in an upper bunk, his face to the wall. Anse was at the big poker table, studying a map spread beside a lamp.

"Your Ma wants you, Barr," Jeff said. He and Anse looked at each other. They knew who had killed Wavell, after watching Barr when Allie Odom, all worried, came rushing with the news he had heard in town.

Barr did not move or acknowledge the message.

"He's tired," Anse said. "He's had a busy day thinking about crops. Why don't you go see Ma, Barr?"

The voice was smooth, but Jeff knew how the implications of the question must have rubbed grit savagely across Barr's nerves.

Barr rolled over. His face was sullen, but his eyes peered down from the gloomy shelf like those of a trapped lobo. "Don't push me too far, Anse. You know I'm stuck with you now."

"Now?" Anse glanced at Jeff. "Why now?"

They all three knew and they were sure that each other knew, Jeff thought, so there was something starkly cruel in this playing on Barr's guilt. There was a wall in Anse Honeywell's brain that blocked away all natural feeling. It troubled Jeff only because he knew he would have to screw his caution down to deal successfully with Anse.

Barr climbed from the bunk. He put on his hat and strapped his pistol belt around him. Anse watched him narrowly, half smiling, and then he said, "No one will ever find out from us that you stood on a hill and put that .44-40 you're so proud of on a man who gave—"

"Shut up!" Barr rushed into the night. Not long afterward the two men in the bunkhouse heard him ride away.

He had nowhere to go, Jeff thought, nothing to do but lean at a gallop into the flow of cold night air, to ride up one hill and down another, and then to return just the same as when he left. He had killed a man and the thought was riding him; he was weak. Jeff nodded toward the house. "She'll corner him one day and get it out of him."

"She might have guessed the truth already, but she won't get anything out of Barr—not now."

"Why'd he do it?"

"The girl who came here one day, remember? I think maybe Barr got some notion about her and Wavell. That's the only thing I can lay it to." Anse shrugged.

For a few moments he remembered his older brother when they had been kids. Barr did the fighting. Barr had taken care of Anse's quarrels. Barr had been a good looking kid, a little broody perhaps. He had been a good looking man until the strain of the last few years put gauntness into his face.

Maybe if he and Bitsy could have been married, if Anse could have figured some way to let him go ahead with his idea of farming . . . No, the way things had developed there had been no room for sentiment in Anse's plan. He had done the right thing.

Anse forgot his brother and gave attention to the map. He ran his palm across it. "Anywhere," he said. "We can go in anywhere now."

"They'll be waiting now."

"They can't cover twenty miles of mountains."

Jeff said, "That Chaunce is smart and hard."

Anse raised his eyes quickly. "You talk like you know him."

"I saw him here. That was enough."

"No," Anse said. "It ain't enough. You slipped, Jeff.

127

You're the Lone Star foreman when I get in. That stands. Get out in the open with me on why you came here."

He had been talking altogether too much since coming to Seven Cross, Jeff thought. When you talked, you were bound to give yourself away; but now he couldn't stop.

"I've been after Chauncey Wade a long time."

"How about Krimble?"

Jeff shook his head.

Once more Anse turned to the map. For several moments he looked at it, and then his deep eyes were on Jeff again. "They were raised together, always been close together, from what I hear."

"I want Wade, tha's all."

"All right. We'll let it go at that."

"Be satisfied about it, Anse."

"I am."

He was lying and Jeff knew it; and he also knew that men whose purposes ran part way in common could lie to each other harmoniously—until their purposes branched from the common stem. So far, he and Anse were together.

Anse tapped the map. "I'm not just sure where to put the next drive."

"You want it to be a fight, or just a nuisance?"

"A nuisance, this time."

Jeff thought he knew Anse's mind fairly well. Anse wanted to sting Krimble into coming out of the mountains and striking somewhere in the hills. Right now the power was against Krimble, but a few bold raids could shift the balance. Krimble would not have to hit too hard to cause hill ranchers like Allie Odom, and others of his stripe, to lose interest in the mountains.

When the two sides were about even, Anse would figure to bring about a showdown that would ruin everybody but himself. It was smart enough, Jeff admitted; he had to admire Anse. But the plan was too slow.

"You can't stall around until Krimble's round-up crew starts drifting in," Jeff said. "That'll be about a month, I judge."

Anse smiled. "That was what Wavell was playing for. By the way, your boy is getting sort of thick with Lone Star. Can you handle him?"

"I can handle him."

"How?"

"He hasn't learned everything he ought to know to get along by himself in the little time he's been away from me. He'll be coming around."

"Yeah? All I had to do was jerk a muscle today and he would have been shooting."

"He would have got you too," Jeff said. "I taught him."

Insects flirted with the lamp. A heavy kerosene odor hung in the silent room as the two men studied each other.

"Shift him toward Callaway," Anse said. "Big George has got it coming for staging that raid too soon."

Jeff nodded. Too soon. Everything was too soon with Anse. Things had to be speeded up. After years of waiting to get at Krimble, each day of waiting was now another year.

"I think I'll fake a drive up Hampson Valley," Anse said, rubbing his finger along the map, "and then we'll put another bunch in at Big Spruce again. Even Alice Krimble won't be able to hold Jim down after that."

Anse might be feinting right here at the table, Jeff

129

thought, loosing easy information to test out Jeff. He might have sensed Jeff's impatience to get the fight going in earnest. One sure way of putting a firecracker under things was to let Krimble know where the next drive would strike his land. You couldn't tell what was in Anse's mind, except a distrust of all men.

Jeff could understand that well enough. He nodded. "Big Spruce might fool him completely."

"Might? I know it will."

Too much talk; a slip. Jeff was now certain that no drive was intended for Big Spruce. Sooner or later a talking man said a few words too many.

Mrs. Honeywell called out, and then she pushed the door open, standing on the threshold with a shawl around her head and shoulders.

"Where did Barr go?"

"To Shepherd's, I think," Anse said. "Didn't he mention something about seeing one of Tol's girls, Jeff?"

"Yeah."

"He rode west," Mrs. Honeywell said slowly. "He rode west like the devil was biting him." Her eyes were bright points in the gloom of her face. "Who killed Ben Wavell, Anse?"

Anse frowned. "Hush that, Ma! I think Callaway did it, but it's not something to talk about."

"You're lying, Anse. The mark of a cloven hoof is deep on your father's land these days. I saw it in the darkness on the way across the yard, glowing in the darkness where Jack Bovee's blood ran out."

Jeff was fascinated by the old woman's tolling voice, but otherwise he was unimpressed. He watched her step back into the darkness and disappear. Half amused he glanced at Anse. Some of the color was gone from

130

Anse's cheeks, and he was staring through the open door.

Well now, that was something, to think the old lady could get to Anse like that.

Jeff went over and closed the door. "When I'm foreman up there," he said, "I'll want a big year-round crew to make sure that what's going to happen to Krimble never happens to us."

"Yeah." Color was returning to Anse's face. "You've got to keep strong. That's what Krimble's wife made him forget." He lost the thought immediately. "You don't suppose she did see something out there? One of the dogs' tracks—or something?"

"No. Women are funny," Jeff said. It was a woman who had ruined Jeff Arbuckle, so he had been telling himself for years, forgetting everything but what he wanted to remember. Let this second woman ruin Jim Krimble now, but the ghost of the first one, through Clay, must be at the kill.

Jeff gave fierce thanks because he had been able to get past his first sight of Krimble, after all the years, without killing the man. Jack Bovee was forgotten. A bullet into him had meant no more to Jeff than the two bullets into the ground, except that the ground could not bleed to wash away Jeff's rage.

Barr came in long after Jeff and Anse were in bed. Jeff heard him undress quietly in the darkness, and then he heard the rustle of the straw-filled mattress when Barr settled into his bunk. After that it was quiet, but Jeff knew Barr was not sleeping.

He was lying there all tense, seeing things in the darkness. The poor weak fool. This whole family was sort of spooky. The mark of the devil's hoof where blood had run upon the ground . . . Jeff yawned and

131

went to sleep.

Once in the night the dogs howled dismally. Barr went running out to curse them into silence. When he came back, Jeff, only half awake, heard him standing bare-footed in the middle of the room, breathing heavily, before he climbed again into his bunk.

The dogs, Jeff thought. *Anse's dogs. Now there was an idea.*

The gather at Callaway's was ready, about twelve hundred cattle, sheep-cropping fields that were already bare, bawling their hunger irritably. Jeff had never seen such a skinny bunch of stuff in one place, not even longhorns after a brutal winter.

He watched Big George ride up to Barr, who was sitting his horse apart from all the others. "This one will be rubbing it in his face!" Callaway said. "How about it, Barr?"

Barr grunted something and moved his horse away.

Anse stood high in his stirrups and waved his arms for everyone to gather on him. There were still twenty men ready to ride with the hillmen's purpose, and Odom was one of them.

They gathered around Anse, their horses jostling. "We'll put the herd into the mouth of Hampson Valley," Anse said. "Whoever's watching the hills for Krimble will sorefoot his horse back to Lone Star to report. By the time they get organized we'll be halfway to Big Spruce. By the time Krimble gets *there*, he won't find anything but cattle spreading out into all those little parks. We'll be long gone."

Anse did not look at Jeff once.

Big George said, "It's all right but it ain't direct. When do we aim to hit Lone Star right in their front yard?"

"When the time is right," Anse said.

Odom moved his glasses up and down and peered around anxiously. "Suppose Krimble decides to hit down here first? I got a wife and kids at home and—"

"With kids it's best to have a wife, Allie." The gravity of Anse's face made the quip hit harder. When the laughter quieted Anse said, "We can't huddle behind a stockade, Odom. My mother is at home alone and I worry about that too, but we got to take our chances."

"If it lays real turrible on your mind, Odom, I'll stay home with your wife." Big George grinned.

Odom stared at the ground when the laughter came again.

"Let's go!" Anse waved his arm.

With wild yells the riders raced away to start the herd. The corner of Jeff's mouth twisted. The fools acted like they were starting three thousand head north from Texas on a real drive, instead of playing duck-on-a-rock like a bunch of bellowing kids.

Befitting his position as commander, Anse did none of the dusty work. He sat looking at the mountains until the herd was strung out, and then he went to the point, motioning for Jeff and Odom to join him.

"I know you're worried, Allie," Anse said. "So am I. The last thing we want is a shooting fight that might draw Krimble down here. You scout in as close as you can to Lone Star. If they catch on to our shift and start men toward Big Spruce too soon, you scoot back and let us know."

"I'm not much at scouting." Odom licked his lips.

He didn't want any part of the whole business, Jeff thought, except a chance to fatten his cattle after someone else did the chores.

"You'll be safe enough," Anse said. "Jeff, you go on ahead and look Sash over. We've got to swing close to there when we head for Big Spruce. If Krimble's girl, or someone else from Lone Star, is hanging around Sash— well, you'll just have to hold them there until there's no chance they can get back and give our play away."

Jeff thought it over while he rode ahead. Anse was giving him a chance to tip off the plan to Lone Star. Ever since Anse had known Jeff's impatience to get the shooting started, Anse had been figuring deep. There was not going to be any ruse at all; the herd was going right up Hampson Valley. Jeff was doggone sure of that.

And Odom—all Anse had done for him was give him a chance to get shot as a spy prowling around Lone Star. Odom was infecting others with his nervousness. The little muskrat-face didn't realize Anse had marked him for a bullet. It would not be Anse's bullet.

Not far from Sash Jeff met Geldien and Clay, driving stripped-down wagons toward the mountains. With a bare nod Geldien glanced at Jeff and drove on. Clay stopped.

A sneer dropped one corner of Jeff's wide mouth. "You look good on that rig, Clay."

The sickness of his last meeting with his father came over Clay. "I'm helping to build something," he said, and he knew Jeff would never understand.

"A cabin. My, that's wonderful, Clay!" Jeff shook his head. "Been thinking of what I told you?"

"No."

Jeff laughed.

Away from his father, Clay could believe what he worked out slowly in his own mind; with his father, as now, he could see nothing but Jeff's cold sureness.

"Who's at Sash now?" Jeff asked.

"Nobody! There's nothing left to burn."

"Still a kid. You figure I'm playing in this penny-ante game, don't you? Anse Honeywell is using a bunch of half-wits, some of 'em with wives and kids. Right now the gather of the last week is headed for Hampson Valley. Krimble is as dumb as the rest.

"About the time he starts skinning up horses in the timber on his way to Hampson Valley, that drive will be near Big Spruce."

Jeff rode on toward Sash. There was a darned good chance now that Clay, having made friends at Lone Star, would pass the word. Krimble would get sucked in, maybe. If that happened Clay wouldn't be so well liked around Lone Star. Jeff knew just how much the displeasure and distrust of people hurt Clay; he was inclined to be savage after being rebuffed. In that, he was his father all over.

Yes, it might help to bring Clay back a little sooner, to return him to the job Jeff had trained him for. You could tell that Clay had been in a torment ever since Jeff told him the lie about being crazy.

As Jeff rode on toward Sash to have a look around for himself, not trusting Clay, whom he considered too stupid to tell anything but the truth, he wondered which one he hated most: Jim Krimble or his son, Kevin.

There was no one at Sash. Jeff settled down behind a hill to watch the place. This waiting was awful because it gave doubt a chance to twist acid-tipped fingers in Jeff's brain. Old Chaunce Wade was no fool. His guesses often were sharper than his nose. He might out-guess both Anse and Jeff.

If a fight built up in Hampson Valley, Krimble would be in it and he might be killed. No, he would not! He had always had the devil's luck. He would not die until

135

Jeff took care of the details, and told Jim Krimble the truth while he lay dying.

Then Clay could be told the truth, so he could suffer too for being the son of Jim Krimble. It was too bad there were not about four generations of them to suffer.

It was all rifle noise. The sounds came distantly across the sullen gray hills in mid afternoon, carrying fear to listeners in a dozen places.

Mrs. Odom walked a little farther into the yard, and her children were drawn to her by the terror of her frozen attitude. "Not Allie, not Allie!" she said under her breath. "Oh why didn't he stay out of it?"

The children cocked their heads toward the mountains.

"That sounds about somewhere near Hampson Valley," one said.

"What's happening up there, Ma?" another asked.

At Seven Cross, Mrs. Honeywell rocked a little faster as she sat with her Bible open on her lap. She closed her eyes and murmured, "Take Anse now, O Lord, take him now, and let Barr come back."

She, too, wondered what was happening.

Jeff Arbuckle stood up and shaded his eyes. His face was a mesh of evil lines as he listened to the tiny cracking sounds.

That long-nosed Chauncey Wade, they had not fooled him for a minute. Jeff wondered if Clay had passed the word along. Most of all he wondered what was happening to Krimble.

"Don't let him get killed," he asked of some vague power that, in moments of helplessness, he considered greater than himself.

Loading timber on a wagon, the Dean brothers stopped with a log part way up their pole ramp. They scowled at each other, and then they looked at Clay and Geldien.

"Krimble must have been set this time," Parley said.

Orley spat. "Somebody's going home the hard way."

The sounds were little tears in Clay's mind. He had argued with himself about telling Lone Star, and then he had asked Geldien's opinion. "It depends on how well you know your father," Geldien said. Lying behind the words, Clay realized, was the thought that Jeff was the Seven Cross man who had killed Bovee.

Clay made his decision; he took one of the work horses and rode toward Lone Star. It was no longer possible for him to tell himself that what happened all around him was not his business. Before he had gone a mile, one of Krimble's men stepped out from a clump of spruce trees.

There was no friendliness in Toby Lashbrook. His pistol was in his hand.

Lone Star was holding its picket line almighty close to the hills these days, Clay thought. He told Lashbrook about Hampson Valley and Big Spruce.

"Who says it's a trick?"

After some hesitation Clay said, "My father."

"Him, huh?"

One Arbuckle, all Arbuckles. Clay saw the hatred. Already his old resentment of distrust was grinding. What if Lashbrook had been a close friend of Bovee's; that still did not cover all his attitude.

Suddenly Clay felt like a dirty spy. He let a little of his anger spill on Lashbrook.

"You'd better let Wade judge it," he said.

"Uh-huh. Wade may think you're something special, Arbuckle, but I don't." Lashbrook gestured with his pistol toward the hills.

All the way back to where his friends were cutting timber Clay tried to come to grips with his own thinking. He had broken from Jeff's narrow way, and had moved with some confidence toward a bigger kind of life. Damned if he was going to let Lashbrook's rebuff start him backing away from life again.

But it was not so easy to meet the revelation Jeff had made the other evening. He guessed that he had better go see Jeff again as soon as possible, and get all the facts and evidence. Crazy. That was a terrible weight to carry on the mind.

Now the distance-muted sounds of rifle fire came through the timber to Clay. In good faith, acting on his own decision, he had tried to let Lone Star know that the drive to Hampson Valley was only a ruse. Jeff must have lied, and Clay had passed along the lie—and Wade, if Lashbrook had told him, had not been fooled at all.

What now was Lone Star's opinion of Clay Arbuckle?

Deadly bitter for a while, Clay fell into old habit: he should have stayed clear of other men's grief. Then he rejected that kind of thinking. Geldien and the Deans had not stayed clear of Nairn's trouble. If a man wanted to be linked to other human beings, he had to accept their troubles and feel a need to help. Wavell had been like that, and even Dutch Holcomb had put his neck out publicly for Nairn.

Clay thought it through, fumbling, worrying. In the end he decided that his own opinion of himself was sound. But the rifles kept sending little jars against his tissue.

"Going strong," Geldien said. "What's happening, do you suppose?"

What Anse Honeywell did not know was that Art Kelley was the only man now sleeping at Lone Star. All others were spread in three camps close to the hills. Before going, Krimble made his wife two promises: not to carry the fight into the hills, and not to kill unless forced to do so. They were his promises, not his wife's exactions; she had wanted much more.

High on a bench, a lookout saw the dust when the herd began to move. It was four miles, around cliffs, down through timber, and across meadows, to another lookout. The warning was flashed in seconds, and then the first spotter sat down, across his lap a mirror that had lately hung in the bunkhouse at Lone Star. He got an envelope from his shirt and once more studied the simple code that would tell him what to do.

That Krimble, he thought, must be half Indian.

Long before the herd neared Hampson Valley, the two flanking camps of Lone Star men, and the lookouts, were moving fast toward where Krimble and Wade waited with two men in the middle camp.

Krimble said to Wade, "He may be faking. That valley narrows down. It's a rough place to move cattle."

"It's also rough for us to get near. If we were starting from home right now we'd never get there before they break out on Sundance Mesa. Maybe Anse figures we're starting from home."

"Maybe," Krimble said. "We'll wait a while."

"With four men, I think we'd better."

Krimble grinned suddenly. "You never used to count so close. Who are you—Will Shertz, figuring accounts?"

Put the two of them together, Clay and Krimble, let them grin at once and anyone would know they were

139

father and son. On the edge of speaking from impulse, Wade again recalled the day Krimble had said it was best one part of his life be wiped away completely.

"Age teaches you to count," Wade said. He got his binoculars from his saddle bags. There was a day, too, when he would have scorned the use of extra eyes.

What with the dust and the shifting of men back and forth on the flanks, he settled for twenty riders. One had gone toward Sash, and another had ridden toward the mountains.

Later, the four men from the south camp came in, driving Allie Odom ahead of them. "He rode smack into us," grizzled Solo Blanchard said. "At first we figured to stone him to death with little pine cones, but . . ." He shrugged.

Standing face to face with physical fear, Odom mustered dignity that he never owned under normal circumstances. He did not fiddle with his glasses or scrub his buck teeth with his tongue. He looked at Krimble's dark, heavy features, and he glanced at Wade's tough, blank expression.

"I finally figured that Anse sent me up here to get killed," Odom said.

Krimble and Wade glanced at each other. They turned away. A cowboy motioned for Odom to get down and sit by a tree. After a while, all of the little man's dignity left him, and he sat there staring fearfully at his boot tips.

The riders from the north camp came in, with their horses skinned and limping. Toby Lashbrook was the last lookout to come in. By then the cattle were stringing out in Hampson Valley.

Wade gave his binoculars to Krimble. "I don't know. Anse is near the mouth of the valley with a half dozen

140

men, and they're holding part of the herd back. They must figure we've seen 'em. They could be faking."

"That Arbuckle," Lashbrook said, "he said it was a fake. He said the herd was going to pull out of there and go to Big Spruce hogback again."

Wade whirled around. "Which Arbuckle?"

"The young one—at Sash."

"How'd he know?"

"His father told him so."

Wade looked at Krimble.

"He rode up on a work horse to tell me," Lashbrook said. "That made it look good, I suppose."

"Where are we now, Chaunce?" Krimble asked.

"I trust Clay," Wade said. "That fellow who claims to be that father of his at Seven Cross, if he's the one I think he is—My God, I must be wrong . . ."

Krimble waited. "You must be a little off. What are you trying to say?"

They had left Jeff Slaughter dying on the ground that foggy day back in Texas. Jim had said something about him getting off too easy, and then they had ridden into the mist.

"What's the matter with you, Chaunce?"

There had always been the rumor that Slaughter had recovered, after two years of being crippled, but any rumor could come out of Texas, big as the winds that blew down there. Wade was a Kentucky man himself.

"Clay's father lied to him," Wade said. "Clay swallowed it. Let's head for the canyon just this side of Sundance. If we catch 'em there we got 'em in a jug."

"I think so too," Krimble said. "I also think Clay Arbuckle lied, right along with his father. You ever seen that father, Chaunce?"

"I heard his rifle that day at Seven Cross," Toby

141

Lashbrook said. "I want to see him." He started toward his horse, and then he stopped to look at Odom. "What about him?"

"Let him sit there and rest," Krimble said. "Give him back anything you took, Solo."

Blanchard tossed a carbine and pistol toward Odom's boots. A brightening of comprehension ran across Odom's face. He rose quickly. "Thanks, Jim! I won't forget this. I'm through with Anse and his bunch right now!"

Lone Star rode away and left Odom still trying to thank them. He might have been a tree, the way they acted. He picked up his pistol and swung the cylinder. Loaded. He worked the lever of his carbine and brass began sliding from the chamber.

He stood there blinking like a wistful beaver; they had not accorded him the status of a man. After a while he rode slowly back toward the valley, away from the last crashing sounds of Lone Star on its way to meet the hill men near Sundance Mesa.

It was slippery riding on the steep grassy slopes just under the mesa. Big George held his horse against the hill and looked across the backs of the cattle to where Barr Honeywell was tightening his cinch on the other side of the narrow valley.

Six other hill ranchers had squeezed through the canyon ahead of the herd, and they were behind Big George. Far yonder, in the broader part of the valley, the other half of the herd was coming slowly.

Anse was an old woman, changing his mind at the last instant, deciding to make the drive this way after all. It was not direct, the whole business. What they ought to—

Big George saw movement on the hill above him, and then he was looking at Jim Krimble, clear and big against the sky.

"Where do you want to turn 'em around, Callaway?"

Big George's mind snapped tight for an instant, but a moment later he was all calculation and cunning. There couldn't be too many of them up there, maybe old frost-eyed Wade . . . Krimble might even be alone. Callaway looked sidewise across the little valley. Barr's right hand was reaching toward his rifle scabbard.

"It looks like you caught us foul, Jim." Big George looked up and grinned. He raked his right heel, on the side away from Krimble, back into the flank of his horse. The animal tried to surge ahead, but Callaway was curbing it at the same time.

For a few seconds it appeared that Big George was having trouble, and during those few seconds he hauled his rifle clear. The horse by then was turned head-on into the slope. Big George fired the first shot with one hand, and knocked Krimble, his pistol half drawn, out of sight at the top of the hill.

The rest was a blasting echo. Big George was lifted from his saddle. He rolled and slid until he bumped the legs of the frightened herd, and then the hooves covered him.

Barr Honeywell's rifle was clear. He scrambled uphill, under the belly of his horse, a split second before bullets whacked the animal. The horse leaped ahead, screaming its agony, and then it crashed and slid downhill, spilling its guts all the way to the hooves below.

Barr sat down on the slope. He waited until a man raised his head to see above the drifting smoke at the top of the hill. Barr shot him through the head. Bullets

143

chunked into the sod around Barr. One whipped the muscles of his right arm. Another tore the top half of his ear away.

He sprang up then, yelling defiance at the mesa. In long leaps he went down the slope toward the panicking cattle. They were spreading now, kicking the summer's dust from the grass, grinding more dust from the bottom of the wash. The motion of frantic cattle breaking from the pressure of the herd and the increasing drift of dust protected Barr.

He dodged stray animals, cursing them and cursing those on the hill, not knowing that he was shouting. Twice he shot steers coming at him head-on. He knelt on the thinly haired belly of one, and shot quite carefully at movement on the hill.

From plunging horses fighting the slope the six hill men farther down the valley were firing at the edge of the mesa. Olin Limberis swung his rifle with one hand motioning for the three men on his side of the valley to follow him straight up the hill.

Half way to the top his horse went down, its nose striking the earth like a hammer stroke. Limberis stepped clear and fired his rifle. A bullet knocked his leg from under him and he began to roll. Still clinging to his rifle, he clawed the grass with the other hand until he stopped. Tol Shepherd reached down and helped him rise to gain a stirrup grip.

Pawing with its forefeet, driving with its hind legs, the horse took them both to the mesa edge, and there Shepherd leaped down to lie beside Limberis. They both began a flanking fire on Lone Star. One man joined them. The last one did not make it.

Across the valley, the other two slanted desperately for an outcrop of granite. One man gained protection behind the rock; the other reached it but did not last to get behind it.

Somewhere below, along the edge of the maddened herd, Barr was still dodging his way, pausing to shoot, reloading once in the middle of confusion.

Over on the Lone Star side Chauncey Wade shook his head at Krimble. "That ain't nothing. It bounced off the shin bone. Your leg's numb, that's all."

"Damned good and numb. Who's left down there?"

"Quite a few. Limberis and Shep and another one made it up this side. There's one behind a rock on the other side. Three are done for, maybe four, because I think the cattle tromped Barr."

"Stop it," Krimble said.

"Hell, there'll be a dozen more coming up in a minute."

"Stop it. Yell out to Shepherd. He's got some sense."

"It ain't good and settled yet, Jim."

"Stop it, I said!"

Wade crawled away. Solo was dead and two men were wounded, and it was just about all Barr's work, Wade figured. He passed the order to stop firing. Toby Lashbrook kept on shooting at the outcrop until Wade pushed his rifle down.

Lashbrook said, "That's Jeff Arbuckle behind the rock, Chaunce. I want—"

"So do I, but that ain't him. Quit shooting."

When the Lone Star rifles were quiet the bawling of the cattle came up like a wave of frenzy. On the slope of the valley the man behind the rock kept feeling the edge of the mesa with lead. Wade kept crawling toward Shepherd until he thought he could be heard above the cattle.

"Shepherd!"

A bullet skimmed the grass above Wade.

"You hear me, Shep?"

"I hear you."

"Got enough?"

Shepherd said, "You ain't won nothing yet, Wade."

"You're on foot. Limberis is hit. We're willing to let you go."

Lashbrook cursed.

After a long pause Shepherd called. "We ain't licked, but we're willing to call it off."

"Then stand up and tell that guy across the way to stop shooting."

Shepherd rose out of the grass, and Wade was surprised to see that he was within easy pistol range of the man. Still holding his rifle, Shepherd waved his hat at the hill man across the valley. The man stopped firing. Lone Star riders began to ease up on their hands and knees.

"Keep down until I say different!" Wade yelled.

Lashbrook rose higher than the others, craning to get a glimpse of the man behind the granite outcrop.

From the dust screen drifting toward the rock a rifle spat. Lashbrook's head snapped back and then he fell forward as if he had been slammed across the back. The long-guns on the hill smashed out again, directed mistakenly at the outcrop. An instant later Barr Honeywell leaped away from the carcass of a steer, sprinted along the hill and flung himself behind the rock.

Shepherd was flat again, and the Lone Star bullets were futile. All they did was grind spouts of dust from the granite outcrop.

Wade crawled back to Lashbrook. Barr's bullet had knocked away part of his cheekbone. The eye on that

146

side was big and staring. Toby Lashbrook would never be a dandy at schoolhouse dances again.

"Quit wasting your fire!" Wade yelled. "Pile up the cattle at the narrow part of the valley, there at the start of the canyon!"

The rifles shifted then and began to cripple steers. Other animals came lunging over the struggling mass. Lone Star poured it on the bottle neck, and soon the way was blocked.

Wade crawled on over to Krimble. "Let's wipe 'em out, Jim!" It should have been done with the first few shots, but everybody had shot at Callaway then. By five minutes Lone Star had missed getting a position above the canyon, where no one could have escaped. "I say wipe 'em out, Jim!"

"Who fired the one that knocked Toby over?"

"Barr Honeywell! I thought he was done."

"How's Toby?"

"Mangled in the face, that's all."

"Stop it, Chaunce." Through the crash of rifles Krimble yelled again. "Stop it, Chaunce!"

Wade cursed a woman, and he cursed the stiffness of his joints as he crawled once more to silence Lone Star rifles, and then he went on toward Shepherd a second time.

Shepherd did not answer. After a while, raising his head cautiously, Wade figured it out. Shepherd and the two with him had crawled back to the edge of the canyon, into the rocks.

Across the way Barr's rifle spoke now and then from behind the rock. Wade heard the other man let out a quavering, triumphant yell. The rest of the hill men were coming up. By now they would be out of the trap and on the mesa. That's where Wade spotted them a moment later. He went back to Krimble.

"Anse won't close in," Krimble said. "He'll clear the men we got trapped and drift away. He don't want a fullout scrap, not right now."

"The hell!" It had not gone very well, Wade thought. "The boys are steadied down some now. We can run Anse and the rest clean to their front doors."

"No, Chaunce. Let them go."

It happened that Krimble had guessed correctly. From the rocks at the canyon rim, where Shepherd and his two companions were, and from the edge of the opposite mesa, the hill men pinned Lone Star down, while Barr and his companions escaped.

Then there was only the bedlam in the canyon where cattle were trapped between the wall of dead beef and the pressure of the herd behind. Those above the barrier were gone now, scattered toward the mountains.

"Maybe Anse is circling back toward our horses," Wade said.

Krimble shook his head. "They're gone. Anse won't go too far in any one pass, not until he's got a cinch."

"If he gets sore—"

"You've never seen him mad, Chaunce." Krimble stood up on one leg. "Let's take care of our hurt. Take Solo back to the ranch. Run the cows that got through back to the hills. I ain't going home just yet, Chaunce."

Wade was looking into the valley at a lump that might be Big George. In the heat of conflict Wade had favored killing every hill man in the country, but now he was tired; tired and a little old. It used to be that he was sure about the things he fought for, or maybe he had not tried to look at his reasons. He was glad now that Shepherd, for one, had got away, even if Shep had been one of the men in the Horseshoe.

148

Wade looked at Solo Blanchard, lying there with his brains on the back of his neck. It was Solo who came in on a crippled horse the day Krimble and Wade gave up their search for Kevin. Solo had ridden from Texas with them, and Solo had squatted in the valley where the Lone Star home place now was, looking up with an unbelieving grin when Jim said, "Right here we'll build a stronghold, and when we own these mountains we'll be so tough that no one can come near here unless we want him to!"

Krimble could not hold a worthless woman, and circumstance had taken his son from him, so now he was going to hold hard to something that could not run away or die, land.

That's the way it had been in a virgin valley when there was no gray in Wade's hair. It was different now. Alice made the change; but anyway, Wade guessed a man could not hold anything for sure. He looked at Lashbrook, coming to now, his eye swelled shut, his jaw all loose and hanging from shock.

Wade thought it was time to feel enraged and full of vengeance, but he was tired. All he felt was a strange sort of wonder about events, and a deep regret that old Solo Blanchard would not be around any more to tell his drawling lies and sing his songs.

Jeff Arbuckle rode along the toe of the mountains on his way back to Seven Cross. They had burned a pile of powder up there. Jeff was worried about Krimble.

He met Geldien hauling a load of logs.

"What happened, Geldien?"

Geldien shook his head and went on past.

Jeff put his horse to a gallop when he saw Allie Odom a little later. Odom was poking along as if he did not care if he got anywhere. He blinked at Jeff as though he did not know him.

"What happened?"

"They fought, I guess," Odom said listlessly.

"Did Krimble—" Jeff checked himself. "Well, don't you know anything about it? You were up that way."

"They caught me—that Solo Blanchard and some others. They let me go." Odom put no emphasis on either statement. "I'm through with this thing, Arbuckle."

"You were through a long time ago, except that you figured the others might make a go of it and you'd be left out."

"That's right," Odom said tonelessly.

"You don't know anything that happened up there?"

"They took me over to the main bunch. Krimble thought the drive up Hampson Valley might be a fake, just like it was supposed to be. They didn't know which way to jump, and then Toby Lashbrook said it was a fake. He said someone told him so."

"Oh? Who told him so?"

"That fellow with Nairn. Why hell, it was your boy." Odom took his mind away from himself and was interested in the conversation for the first time. "He said that you told him. Wade said if you said it, then it was a lie for sure. So Lone Star lit out for Sundance Mesa."

Odom's apathy returned. "They didn't even talk to me. They threw my carbine and pistol on the ground. They didn't even bother to take the cartridges out."

Jeff's mind was working coldly. That Clay—Jeff had overlooked the fact that the idiot had gone out into society and learned to shoot his mouth off three ways from the middle. Jeff had figured, if Clay passed the word on at all, that he would merely tell what Jeff had

150

said, and not blab for fifteen minutes.

It gave Jeff his first real worry about Clay; the fool was slipping farther away than Jeff had thought. A little freedom—Jeff had been forced to allow him that because Clay was building up inside when they reached South Fork.

A little freedom then so Jeff might be able to allow none at all later. It would still work out. Clay had been broken right, controlled all the way. Jeff could still get him back for the big play, but he would have to hurry events. Anse certainly would not hurry.

Right now there was something demanding more immediate attention.

"Hold up a minute, Odom. My cinch is loose."

Odom stopped, staring at the neck of his horse. "I might have been a kid that didn't count for nothing," he said.

Jeff swung down and drew his pistol when his feet touched ground. He shot Odom. Jeff dropped his pistol and grabbed the cheek strap of the bridle when the horse leaped. With the other hand he held Odom in the saddle. When the horse was merely side-stepping nervously, Jeff used both hands to hold the weight that was coming down on him.

Allie Odom never left his mount. He was across the saddle, lashed with his own rope when Jeff slapped the horse away.

Looking at his tracks afterward, Jeff thought it was unlikely anyone would bother to unravel the trail; especially not when the man who came home across his saddle had been sent to spy on Lone Star.

The timber cutters could not have seen, here behind a hill. They might have heard the shot, but this had been a day of gunfire. Lone Star had killed Odom. Anse would say so, even if he guessed otherwise. It should be a long time before he found out that Jeff had done exactly as Anse thought he might do in sending word to Krimble about the cattle drive.

Jeff blew the dust from his pistol and reloaded. It was not his way to leave sign behind him, but he was driven by the need to find someone who could tell him about Krimble's part in the fight. With his boot toe he gouged a hole deep enough so no hoof would cup it out again, and into it he dropped Odom's glasses and a forty-five shell.

For a while there were dark spots on the road, where dust had rolled itself around dripping blood; and then Odom's horse had cut away on a direct line toward home.

His luck was running pretty good, Jeff thought. If he could just bump into Anse's dogs somewhere up the road, and toll them toward the mountains a short piece . . . They sometimes ranged wide. But the dogs were not out today. Jeff did not see them until they came barking down the valley of Seven Cross to meet him.

Chauncey Wade was more tired than ever when he led the Lone Star fighters into the home valley. He hoped that Alice Krimble would look out and see Solo Blanchard coming in like that, and Lashbrook hanging to his saddle horn, with his face a mess. The other two wounded were not so bad off; one, with a bullet-gashed arm, had volunteered to stay at a lookout post.

Wade hoped she would look, and see what the price of defense was; but he knew she would not see if she looked.

Vanita ran from the house. "Where's Dad?"

"At the cabin on Prower's Meadow."

Vanita glanced at Solo, and then she looked at Lashbrook, who grinned through the caked blood on his face.

"Did you smash them, Chaunce?" she asked.

"We hurt 'em some." Wade swung down. There was something distasteful in talking to a woman about the fight; and something worse in the way Vanita kept looking at him. By God, she ought to be trying to do something for Lashbrook, who used to take her to all the dances, instead of standing there wanting information.

"Who'd you hurt?" she asked.

"Callaway is dead. Two others. Shep got Limberis clear after we hit him."

"The Honeywells?"

"They wasn't in it—right at first. I mean, Anse wasn't. Barr was. He got away." He had done most of the damage too, damn him.

"Then nothing is settled." Vanita went back to the house.

Wade helped Lashbrook off his horse. "I guess we're failures," Lashbrook said. He watched Vanita striding up the graveled walk, and he spoke bitterly from sickness and something else. "I took her to her first dance." He felt his face. "I wonder if she'll go to the next one with me?"

"Shut up!" Wade helped him into the bunkhouse.

Wade was not surprised when one of the women came down a little later and told him that Mrs. Krimble wanted to see him.

She was standing back from one of the big windows, looking at the mountains. She must have been there, Wade thought, when they rode in.

"Sit down, Chauncey."

153

Wade stood just inside the door. She did not look at him.

"The mountains, Chauncey—have you ever thought how big and peaceful they are? None of the petty savageness that races all around them ever affects their appearance. They will be there, just as they are now, when all of us are gone."

"Yeah."

After a while she said, "Jim went to one of the other places, Vanita says."

"Yeah."

"Why?"

She knew. She just wanted a man's viewpoint, so she could forget it as soon as she had it.

Wade said, "He wanted to look at some cattle."

"You're misleading me again, Chaunce."

"By God!—excuse me, Alice—if you saw what just came through the yard—"

"I saw."

"Well, then?"

Vanita came into the room. "The worst of them got away. If you let Dad do—"

"Be quiet, Vanita," Mrs. Krimble said. "You've fallen to the general level of the savagery all around you. I know it, but I want you to be quiet about it in my presence. You go down there and see about that boy you used to dance with. Go right now, Vanita."

Wade watched Vanita go out. Alice could make that girl hop, even if no one else could.

"You haven't forgotten that I want to talk to Jeff Arbuckle, have you, Chaunce?"

"No."

"When?"

"I haven't had a chance to breathe lately!"

154

"Tomorrow morning I am going to South Fork. If you don't bring or send that man to me, I will go see him at Seven Cross. I should call on Amanda Honeywell anyway. It's been two months since I visited her. She is a gentlewoman, Chaunce, and she is too proud to come up here—now."

"All right. I'll get Jeff Arbuckle to South Fork, some way. If I had my say, I'd take him there just the way you seen Solo Blanchard a minute ago!"

"You don't mean that, Chaunce."

Wade's face was now lined with all the bitterness that he had not felt after the fight at Sundance Mesa. For once, the steady, gentle sadness of the look Alice Krimble bore on him did not change anything inside him or on his face.

"I depend on your word, Chauncey."

Wade left before he burst into a futile explanation of views she would never allow herself to admit.

Silent men were standing around the bunkhouse poker table, watching Lashbrook and Vanita. She had washed the grime and blood from the puncher's face, and now the sight of the wound was enough to sicken a man.

"It really isn't bad, Toby," Vanita said. She looked at Wade. "But he should be taken to a doctor, don't you think?" She patted Lashbrook's good cheek. "Don't you worry, Tobe, you'll still be the handsomest man in the country."

Lashbrook grinned. Like an idiot, Wade thought. Women. Wade decided he had been a very lucky man to stay single all these years.

The buggy was ready to go the next morning, just when the sun began to slant over the mountains that cradled the green valley. Over there where the big star stood was about the place where Solo had grinned at Krimble's words. In those days the beaver ponds had run clear back to where the lower corrals now stood.

Wade took a good look all around. You couldn't tell; he might not see this again. He guessed there was not so awful much changed since the old days, just the people who lived here. The mountains were the same, just as Alice Krimble had said; they would always be the same.

This morning there was a new grave in the tiny burying ground at the edge of the spruces. Alice had been there in the sunset when they put Solo away. Not once did she look at the two little mounds that covered the twin boys she and Krimble had lost a year after their marriage.

Lashbrook's face was half covered with white cloth. He was running a fever but he smiled when he helped Mrs. Krimble into the buggy. He got in beside her. Vanita had the lines.

"Go ahead," Wade said. "I'll catch up."

Art Kelley was getting sullen. He was the first Lone Star man to have suffered, and ever since they had kept him home taking care of the barn. So now Wade said to him, "You'll find Jim at the cabin on Prower's Meadow. Tell him who's gone to town. Tell him I think the man at Seven Cross is Jeff Slaughter."

When the buggy reached the bottom of the last grade to the hills Vanita started to turn toward Sash. "Not that way," her mother said.

"It's not much farther. I thought we'd go by and see Clay for a minute."

"Not today, please," Mrs. Krimble said.

"I'm going down," Wade said. "I'll catch you before you get to town. You're not afraid to drive across—"

"There is nothing to be afraid of, Chaunce," Mrs.

156

Krimble said. "However, that isn't the way to Seven Cross."

"Don't worry about Seven Cross." Wade was worrying plenty about the place. "I'll get there—or something."

Lashbrook was not feeling so chipper now, but he gave Wade a fevered, surprised look and said, "If you're going there, I'd better—"

"Drive on, Vanita," Mrs. Krimble said. "Before Mr. Lashbrook becomes heroic."

The workers at Sash were raising the last round of logs on the walls of the house. A load of lumber was stacked clean yellow in the yard. Down in the hayfield the mower borrowed from Lone Star sent back a faint clatter.

"Well, Chaunce," Geldien said, "I see you got out in one piece, How's Krimble?"

"Fine."

"We heard he had his leg shattered."

"Bumped a little," Wade said. "What else did you hear?"

"Me 'n Orley rode around last night and picked up the news," Parley Dean said. "We heard you lost Solo and two others."

"Just Solo," Wade said curtly.

"Big George is dead," Parley said. "There was no doubt about that. I seen him go by when Shepherd was bringing him in by lantern light. My God! After that, Shep took Limberis to town—he's got a busted knee. Klingensmith and Allred got it, and Odom—I didn't care much about the way you fellows done him, Wade."

"Odom? What about him?" Wade asked.

"His horse brought him into the yard, while his wife was standing there."

Wade shook his head. "We didn't kill Odom. Solo caught him trying to Indian around, and we turned him loose."

"Somebody got him," Geldien said.

Wade's face was as bleak as old granite. "Someone got Sam Andrews, too, and Lone Star got the blame for that." He looked at Clay. "We turned Allie Odom loose."

"It's one hell of a mess," Orley Dean said. "I'm glad we had sense enough to get out of it."

Their thinking put a heaviness on them all. Geldien broke into the silence on a lighter vein. "Guess who's down there on the mower, Wade."

Wade glanced toward the field, but his mind was elsewhere.

"Billy Smithers," Geldien said. "Dutch Holcomb sent him out. He said he could work his bar bill out on that hay, or never get another drink in the Horseshoe. By gosh, you'd be surprised at how well old Billy's doing. The old cuss was raised on a farm."

"Holcomb sent that lumber, too," Parley said.

Wade nodded, but Clay doubted that he had heard the words.

"See you a minute, Clay?" Wade asked.

Standing by Nairn's fire-wrecked mower, Wade asked another question. "Did you ever know a man named Slaughter?"

Clay could not remember ever knowing anyone by that name. Once more he was disturbed by the press of unknown thoughts behind Wade's odd scrutiny.

"Mrs. Krimble wants to talk to your father. I promised her to get him to go to South Fork. I think, Clay, the minute I see your father, him and me are going to try to kill each other."

"Why?"

"I'm asking you to see if you can't get him to go to town to see Alice Krimble."

"Do you know my father?"

"Yeah, I sure do, but you don't."

For an instant Clay thought there was some subtle significance in the bald statement, and then he realized it was the truth as he knew the truth. "I'll try," he said.

On the way to Seven Cross doubts and fears were a shadowy pack of wolves stalking Clay's mind.

A rider came from the mountains, angling ahead of Clay toward Seven Cross. The man went up a hill and dipped behind another, and then he waited on the next hill. It was Jeff.

The fine green lines of evil were easier to see this time. Tough-mouthed, silent, Jeff waited for Clay to speak.

"Wade says he turned Allie Odom loose. Geldien met you at the toe of the mountains about the time Odom must have been going home. Did you do that, Jeff?"

"Chauncey Wade was always about the biggest liar in the world," Jeff said. "Now if it was you, seeing someone you didn't like, that streak of killer madness in you—"

"You could have lied about that too, Jeff. Odom was there when Toby Lashbrook told Lone Star what you told me. You couldn't afford to have Odom tell Anse and the others—"

"You're simple, Clay. You always was—until your craziness strikes you. Wade has taken you in. I will tell you something, though. I just tolled Anse Honeywell's dogs into the mountains and shot them. Anse is going to be like you when he finds out Lone Star killed his dogs. He's going to be killer-crazy, Clay."

159

"You're the crazy one, Jeff."

"Things are moving too slow. They would have been stalled, after the fight yesterday." Jeff grinned. "But now Anse will go for a showdown. It was better than shooting his mother and his brother. Anse wouldn't have batted an eye about that, no more than when he badgered Barr into killing Wavell."

"Barr did!"

"You've been stupid down there in your hayfield, Clay."

"I'm going to see Barr."

"There you go, always wanting to kill somebody. No, Clay, you just leave Barr alone. Try for once to think with your head. I spent a lifetime trying to make a man out of you, instead of a cold-blooded crazy killer."

"Stop saying I'm crazy!"

"It gets to you, doesn't it? I know. I licked the same feeling once myself, and I can do the same for you; but you've got to stick with me, Clay."

"I'm through with you, Jeff."

"Then why'd you come looking for me?"

"To tell you that Alice Krimble wants to see you in South Fork right away."

"Krimble's wife, huh?" Jeff's eyes went down to slits. "Why?"

"I don't know."

The cold silence of Jeff's face spoke of thoughts coiling and uncoiling. "I'll go," he said.

Clay started to swing his horse around.

"If you go with me, Clay."

"What for?"

"It's time you knew about yourself. I'll ride into Seven Cross just long enough to tell Anse about some Lone Star man I seen shooting at his dogs, and then

160

we'll head for town."

"She was a beautiful woman, your mother." Clay was startled by Jeff's tone and by the fierce possessive glint in his eyes. "Krimble and me grew up together in Kentucky. There were a lot of us that went out to Texas after the war. I should have guessed it, Clay, but I was busy building up the ranch for her and you—and Krimble was busy coming around when my back was turned.

"There's been times when I blamed her, but it wasn't her fault. Krimble had a way about him. He was a handsome devil, and always after some woman. You were about five when he started a drive to Kansas. I was off south, buying cattle. They took you along with them.

"It was one hell of a rainy summer. I caught up with them at the Washita, but I was too late. There'd been a stampede. Marta was killed in the wagon without a chance of getting clear. I found you a day later wandering along the river.

"Krimble never even went back to that wagon for three days, Clay. He was too busy, him and Wade, trying to gather up his scattered herd. I took you on up into Oklahoma and left you with some folks to raise, and then I set out after Krimble.

"I finally caught him. Between him and Wade they shot me five times and left me for dead. It was two years before I could walk again. I went looking again, without any luck. Later on, I picked you up and we've been looking for Jim Krimble ever since. Now we've got him, and he's got to suffer, Clay."

Shocked into silence, Clay tried to superimpose the present upon the past; it was the past that came through most strongly, discoloring the present, ruining the future.

"That was a long time ago, Jeff. I don't know—"

"It was yesterday. I've lived with it ever since. What else could I do? I tried to protect you all I could, and sometimes I thought maybe I could forget the whole thing, but it wouldn't work."

How could a man forget it? Clay thought. He had never known his mother to remember her, and his father had been thrust upon him with a jolting impact; and now he could understand some of the reasons for his lonely life.

"You must feel the same as me," Jeff said. "Now that you know."

Krimble and Chauncey Wade? Wade was a friend now.

"There couldn't be some mistake?" Clay asked.

Jeff's look was hard and steady—and pitying.

"But it was a long time ago!"

"She was a beautiful woman, your mother. God forgive me for blaming her at times for what happened."

"It must have been partly her fault," Clay said.

Jeff shook his head. "I talked to a man who was on that drive. He said she wanted to go back, after she realized what she was doing. He said she was tied in the wagon the night of the stampede."

"Oh God!"

By the time they reached South Fork, Clay's face was set and expressionless. They took their horses to Frost's livery. "Wait here until I talk to Krimble's wife," Jeff said, "I wonder who he stole her from?"

At the edge of the aspens Anse Honeywell buried Bull and Champ and Como. He slashed the edge of the shovel against a tree and then he hurled the tool away;

162

and after that he stood there gaunt and stooped, with tears on his face.

Riding down from searching the hill above, Barr paused in uneasy wonder, remembering that Anse had not wept when their father was laid away. Barr had been recovering slowly from a variety of emotions; now he decided for the second time not to follow his brother any farther.

"I think he lied," Barr said. "I didn't find no tracks up there. I think that Arbuckle done it himself."

"I remember when they were little roly-poly pups, dragging boots— What'd you say, Barr?"

Barr repeated his opinion.

Quite slowly Anse sat down. With one hand he smoothed the earth that covered Bull, the biggest and the loudest of them all.

Barr sat his horse uneasily, waiting. "I seen Krimble break out of the mountains a while ago. He headed straight across the hills. Art Kelley was with him."

South Fork, Anse thought. Now was the time to hit Lone Star and burn it out. Wade was gone too. Someone had seen him riding beside a buggy with the Krimble women in it, heading toward South Fork. There would be just about enough men left at Lone Star, and about enough in the hills, with a stomach left for fighting, to bring about a ruinous showdown.

There it was, set up, everything that Anse had planned for so carefully.

"There's no sign of any rider up there like Jeff said?"

Barr shook his head.

Jeff Arbuckle then. Anse looked at the three mounds. "Shepherd and two others went in with Limberis last night. Get the rest, Barr, and meet me in South Fork. We'll take care of everything there."

163

"I'll round 'em up, but I ain't going in, Anse."

Anse rose. "Jeff Arbuckle went there."

"Let him go where he pleases. I'm through."

"No, Barr." The tears were drying on Anse's cheeks. "Wavell was too well liked for you to be through."

Fury whitened Barr's features. Anse turned away from him and got his horse and rode down the hill. Anse had no doubts that Barr would obey.

At Seven Cross Mrs. Honeywell asked, "Where'd you leave Barr, son?"

"Barr! Barr! Jeff Arbuckle murdered my dogs and lit out for town, and you sit there worrying about Barr getting dust in his eyes or a cut on his finger!"

"I worry about you too, Anse. You were the youngest. I've asked the Lord—"

"Ask Him where Barr is then, and leave me be!" Anse cleaned and oiled his pistol, and then he wiped the oil away carefully. He rode toward South Fork.

After a while Amanda Honeywell went to the barn to harness the buggy team. She walked carefully around the place in the yard where Jack Bovee had crumpled from the saddle. For those with eyes to see the mark of the cloven hoof was still there in the dust.

Anse Stonewall Jackson Honeywell had been the youngest, born on a proud day here in the valley. The hills had been all rippling green then, and the valley deep with grass.

"We've got a boy, 'Manda! We got another boy!"

As if she hadn't known.

Now Amanda Honeywell made long work of harnessing the buggy team. The straps were stiff, and went into the buckles only after great effort. Twice she leaned her face against old Sally's shoulder, moving her lips slowly.

Hard Frost slipped out of the back door of his livery stable and went down the street to unburden his mind at Will Shertz's general store.

"He's just sitting there on a box near the harness room," Frost said. "I tried to be pleasant but he looked at me like he didn't hear me."

"What's he waiting for?" Shertz asked.

"I don't know. There—"

"Where's the other one his father?"

"In the hotel." Frost looked at his watch. "Three hours and eighteen minutes."

"I don't like it!" Shertz scowled at his clerk, who was going over freight bills. "Krimble just came in, with that lanky puncher the Honeywells beat up. Wade and them went into Dutch's place to see Nairn. Shepherd and two other hill ranchers were there with Limberis." He paused. "Nothing happened though."

"See there!" Frost said. "If it wasn't for Anse Honeywell—"

"I tried to do what I could about him, didn't I? How'd I know this young Arbuckle was just a hay hand after all?"

"Oh, no, Will! You go up and look at him sitting on that box and see if you think he's a hay hand now."

"What we need around here is some law," Shertz said irritably. "Toby Lashbrook has got half his face shot away and he won't go to bed. He keeps making talk about this Jeff Arbuckle that killed Jack Bovee. Pretty soon—"

"Now we got something!" Frost said. "Look there!"

Anse Honeywell was riding up the street. He stopped in front of the Horseshoe, looked casually at Wade's horse, and went inside.

Shertz and Frost crowded the front window of the store as if afraid to take their eyes away from the Horseshoe.

After a while Frost said, "Now that beats hell! The walls of the place ought to start coming apart."

"Maybe not. Shepherd said they called some kind of truce at the fight in the mountains. Just the same, I'm glad they're all not crowded in here."

"That Clay Arbuckle is still the worst," Frost said. "You ought to see him sitting there all frozen-faced, with his mind a thousand miles away."

They watched Bitsy Miller come out of the Horseshoe and walk straight to Frost's stable. Her dress was a bright splash against the gloom inside the big doors. Then she disappeared.

Frost and Shertz looked at each other.

"Now what?" Shertz asked. "That fellow is on one side, at least friendly to it, and his father works for Anse. They rode in together though. I don't like the whole feel and smell of this thing. Why did they have to haul their fight in here?"

"Billy Nairn would like to see you, Clay."

Billy Nairn. He was a shadow from the past, like Sash, like Geldien and the Dean boys and Wavell, the friends Clay had once known. Now they lay far distant in his mind, while the remote past brought to life by Jeff was a sheet of living fire. Clay looked at Bitsy and nodded slightly.

"What's the trouble, Clay?"

For a moment he formed linkage with the present. This was the woman he had told about the stampede. She was a serious, pretty little woman, and he had liked her. He considered the thought but not the possibility of

166

telling her about Krimble and the past.

And then he tried to forget her entirely.

Her low voice and her presence kept pushing against him. She was Bitsy Miller, the first person who had been friendly to him in South Fork; but what did that mean now?

"What's the trouble, Clay?"

Anse Honeywell had gone into the Horseshoe. He was of the immediate past, which was now the forgotten past. Krimble was also in the Horseshoe, and pretty soon he would come out and walk up or down the street.

Tied in the wagon . . . With all the terror surging loose that night, she was tied in the wagon.

In the gloom of a livery stable, with Jingo, a dead man's horse, stomping in a stall across from him, Clay sat on a box and sweated out another nightmare; but this time he was wide awake, and his face did not twist and he made no outcry.

"Krimble talked to Tol Shepherd, Clay. There's some hope that there won't be any more fighting."

The hooves pounded on in Clay's brain, and then they were gone; but he knew they would turn and come back again and again, forever—until Krimble was dead.

Bitsy was there, unafraid, troubled. She talked but her voice was nothing. All the lonely coyotes of Clay's life gathered in a mighty chorus, calling for vengeance.

"Don't you want to see Billy?"

Clay nodded, or he might have shaken his head; he did not know or care. He asked one question. "Is Krimble still in the Horseshoe?"

"Yes, he—" She studied his face. "Clay! No, Clay! You have nothing against Jim Krimble."

"Go away, Bitsy."

"They weren't right! People said you came here on a

trail, or to hire into the trouble. They weren't right, Clay! What's changed you now?"

After she had left her last question was like a triangle of thought trying to settle somewhere in Clay's mind. It was all that he remembered of Bitsy's being with him.

He saw Vanita come out of the hotel and go to Mrs. Archer's millinery store. She was selfish. She used a man's directness to disarm, and then she retreated behind a woman's purpose. She was the woman Clay might have loved, knowing that she could have made him miserable as well as happy.

Her going into the millinery store was like her disappearing beyond the horizon of Clay's life.

Someone came in the back door, walking quietly along the dampened floor toward Clay, who for an instant assumed that it was Frost; and then he remembered that the liveryman was still in the general store. Clay leaped to the open doorway of the harness room, his pistol ready.

"That's better, Clay." Jeff came on past the stalls. Nothing seemed to move on his face but after he looked closely at Clay, old Jeff was pleased.

"He's still in Dutch's place," Clay said. "Krimble, I mean. He rode in, and then Anse a while ago."

"I seen them. Anse should have gone to Lone Star. He would have, if I could have taken time to fake sign out there where I killed his dogs."

They watched a buggy coming down a distant gray hill.

"Ma Honeywell." Jeff laughed softly. "She saw the devil's sign where I killed one of Krimble's men."

Even through the blinding curtain of his own purpose there came to Clay an impression of terrible evil. He realized that Jeff was talking far more than usual, that

168

the words must be fragments spinning off a fearful tension.

"Why'd you shoot Bovee?"

"To keep from killing Krimble the easy way."

"Did Bovee start to draw?"

"No, you fool!"

There was no sense in it. Clay looked at his father's face. The waiting silence of the features could not cover the popping lava pits inside. Old doubts about Jeff returned.

Jingo moved restlessly in the stall.

"How about Allie Odom?"

"What about him?"

"Did you kill him?" Clay asked.

"Sure. He overheard that I was the one who sent you to warn Lone Star about the cattle drive."

"You really didn't want to warn Krimble, did you?"

Jeff was watching the Horseshoe, but now he looked at Clay for just a tick of time, and in that instant Clay thought he saw behind the wrinkled face into terrifying blackness: a father's hatred of his own son. Jeff did not answer the question.

"Maybe I understand how you feel about Krimble," Clay said slowly. "But why did you hurt so many others to—"

"I wanted to see him ruined. I sized this fight up the first day I rode out to the hill ranches. To help it along I killed that fellow—what was his name?—Andrews. Now I want to see Jim Krimble crawling on the ground snake-high, the way I had to crawl down there in Texas."

Clay was as sick as he had been one day in Nairn's hay field. He sat down on the box, looking at the ground just inside the play of sunlight.

Jeff talked with a vicious exuberance. "Krimble is ruined now, but he don't know it. Anse is in there talking peace, him and Shepherd, and all the time Barr is leading a bunch to wreck Lone Star. I want Krimble to know that before he dies. I want him to know several things, him and Chaunce Wade.

"We'll move when Anse breaks away from Krimble. I'll take care of Anse. Krimble is your job, Clay."

"You knew Krimble was coming here?"

"I guessed it, yes, when word come to Seven Cross that his women were headed to town. Break his arms first, Clay. Mess up his guts—and then I want to talk to him while he lays there."

"Did you talk to his wife?"

"No, you fool! I sat in a room up there, watching this place, watching the saloon. We've got him now! You've been trained all your life to pay Krimble for what he did to both of us."

Krimble did nothing to me, Clay thought. *My father has done everything to me*. There was no scorching rage left. Clay was awed by the lack of wholeness of everything that had touched his life before he broke away from Jeff. The full meaning of some of the thoughts Wavell had spoken and some of Bitsy's sentences came to him now.

"You didn't even intend to talk to Mrs. Krimble, Jeff. You just wanted to get me here in town."

"That's right."

Clay moved his head slowly, still looking at the ground. "I won't do it."

"Yes, you will." Jeff was coldly certain. "This is what I raised you for. You've got my blood in you to back you up. You'll do it, Clay."

"Like father, like son." They were words with

170

impression only and not true meaning, but they hammered hard.

Jeff started to speak again. His voice stopped on a curse.

Horses were coming from the hills to the west.

South Fork residents had been clinging close to their doorways. Now the fat butcher ran to the Horseshoe. Soon afterward Anse and Shepherd came out with Doc Covert, who kept pointing at the saloon, plainly telling Anse to keep trouble away from where the wounded were. A few businessmen edged out on the walk, ready to leap back to their stores.

Jeff ground his teeth. "That's Barr, with a bunch of fools! Now we can't get at Krimble for a while!"

The riders walked their horses into town, twelve of them. Anse and Shepherd were now in the middle of the street. Covert went back to the saloon.

Toby Lashbrook's bandages were snow-white in the sunshine when he stepped from the Horseshoe with a glass of whiskey in his hand. He watched the riders dismounting down the street. He drank the whiskey and tossed the glass toward them. Krimble and Wade came out and forced him inside again.

It was Shepherd now who was arguing with Anse. His hands raised toward the riders, as if signaling peace, Anse kept nodding; but a little later Shepherd jerked away angrily. He led his horse toward the edge of town, and the gesture said that he was stepping aside.

Anse turned once and looked at Frost's livery stable. Carrying rifles, Barr's group trotted behind the buildings on the right, and thus they came abreast of the Horseshoe, gathering behind the Comet Cafe.

The cook, and a waiter ran out and sprinted up to Shertz's store.

"They're going to box him in!" Jeff's face was hideous. He ran into the saddle room and got his rifle.

When he returned Clay lunged up from the box and twisted the rifle from his father's hands. Jeff was flung to the stable floor. He crouched there, grinding his teeth like an animal.

"If you want Anse, walk down there," Clay said.

"He might kill Krimble!"

"The back of the saloon is logs." Nairn was in the Horseshoe, helpless. Bitsy and Wade and Dutch were there. For the first time without having to reason, Clay felt his linkages of friendship demanding action; but he did not know yet what the action should be.

Mrs. Honeywell had left her buggy down the street, near the bakery. She came from the building and walked in the dust toward Anse. He had started toward the Comet but now he waited. To whatever she said he seemed to be listening with great patience.

With his back to the silent saloon, he waited, listening; and then he took his mother's arm and helped her to the walk in front of the Comet. He pointed up the street. He left his mother on the walk and went inside. If his back had crawled because of the men in the saloon, nothing in Anse Honeywell's behavior indicated the slightest tension.

Mrs. Honeywell disappeared at the side of the Comet. She would see Barr now, Clay thought. Moments later part of the force behind the building left that position and crossed the street below the Horseshoe.

"They're boxing Krimble in!" Jeff cried. He was still on his hands and knees on the stable floor, where he had landed from his struggle with Clay over the rifle.

Mrs. Honeywell came out to the walk again. She moved aimlessly, as if lost. She wandered to the

172

sheriff's office and tried the door, and then she stumbled to the front of the Comet once more and sat down wearily on the edge of the walk.

Clay had never seen her any closer than she was at the moment, but now he started toward her. Jeff cursed him. Before Clay had run ten steps Barr came to the walk and lifted his mother to her feet. At the same time the doors of the Horseshoe opened and Bitsy ran across the street. Mrs. Honeywell turned away from her son then; she went with Bitsy toward the hotel.

For several moments Barr stood looking at the dance-hall girl in her bright calico, at the old woman in a sunbonnet and long black dress. Amanda Honeywell was no larger than the woman who had her arm around her.

With a sudden violent motion Barr swung around and went behind the building again.

Now it was almost set. And now, when it might be too late, Clay knew at last what he was going to do. He went back to Jeff. "I'm going down there in a minute, Jeff."

"You fool! We can't do anything until it starts, and then we'll pick off enough hill ranchers to save Krimble's hide. We can work down behind the buildings—"

"There's nothing in your head but getting at Krimble, is there? You don't care how many—"

"That's been my life! It's yours too."

"No, Jeff. It never was my life. You handed me something today that stunned me, and for a while you pushed your thinking on me, just like you've always tried to do. I was going to kill Krimble, but now I'm going down there and try to stop that whole fight."

"I'll kill you the first step you take, before I say to go." It was there now. Clay saw it beyond all doubt: his

173

father hated him as much as he hated Jim Krimble. From the flashing memory of all the times he had caught the same expression on Jeff's face across the flames of lonely campfires, from the mornings he had wakened to see Jeff watching him unguardedly, Clay now recognized the full meaning of his relationship with his father.

Clay had walked in the reeking filth of vengeance all his life, not knowing it.

"You can shoot me, Jeff," he said, "but I'm going to start."

There was no bluff on either side. Slowly, Jeff brought his features under control. "It can't be done, but I know how you feel."

He never knew how I felt, and he never cared how I felt.

Clay held no thought of atonement for what he and Jeff had done. He was going down the street because he had attached his life to new-found values, and was willing to act on the principles he had discovered.

"You're crazy, Clay. That's the trouble now." Jeff nodded. "You've got one of your brainstorms."

"You can't scare me any more with that. It was part of the squeeze you put on me, but I don't believe it now."

Clay saw that he had wrenched another weapon from his father, perhaps the deadliest one of them all.

Jeff's mouth relaxed. He tried to draw a thoughtful expression to his eyes, but the eyes were too bright; and from underneath everything he put on the surface the evil and cunning came to Clay like a bad odor.

"Maybe I did go too strong in some ways, Clay. I was so taken with myself I made it bad for you, but we can't change all that now. I'll try to make it up to you some way, but first we've got to smash Krimble."

"No, Jeff. Those lost years are yours, not mine."

"We'll take over Lone Star! Think of that! We can do it. We'll handle Anse and then we can do what he's intended to do all the time. Think of it, Clay—Lone Star!"

Clay backed away one step. He knew that when he turned his back fully and started down the street, his father would shoot him; and so Clay planned to edge out even with the line of the sliding doors, and then to leap to the corner of the building.

He eased back another step and then looked over his shoulder at the street. All was silence there. Men not in the fight were huddled in their doorways. Most of them were looking up the street, instead of toward the Horseshoe.

"Don't do it, Clay. I'll get you on the first jump."

There was one course now: disable Jeff and take his weapons. Jeff knew that too. They pinned the fact between them with their eyes, teacher and student of pistol death. Clay thought he had an even chance, no more.

And then he knew he could not take the chance. He would have to kill Jeff. The anguish of all the little coyotes of the world mourned through the emptiness in Clay, crying, *He's your father!*

Outside, near the sliding door on Jeff's right, straw rustled, whispering on a windless day. Then silence.

Jeff tried to look through wood. He glanced down the street at men who were staring in the wrong direction. He tilted his head toward the source of the sound outside, and then he drew his pistol and signalled for Clay to take the left side of the doorway.

The Honeywells were coming in along the doors.

Their pistols were ready. Jeff's leap into sunlight caught Anse by surprise. Time made a little tick before he fired. Jeff shot as soon as there was human form in sight. His bullet threw Anse back one long step. Jeff staggered too, not from the bullet that barely cut his arm, but from the lead Barr put into his back.

Out of the quick savagery only one impression came to Clay. He had stepped to the edge of the left door. His pistol was lying close to the boards, looking right into Barr's face. The barrel made a tiny dip that would mean a shoulder shot. Clay pulled the trigger.

But Barr was already crumpling. Jeff had turned and was driving bullets into Barr. With a frown on his face, with his deep set eyes staring, Barr Honeywell went down, and Clay knew that his bullet had served only to spin the man sidewise.

Anse was dying but he moved a little, pushing his face against the little pile of straw that had betrayed him. Jeff shot him twice.

"Krimble! Krimble!" Jeff whimpered. Holding the growing weight of his pistol in both hands, he ran down the street. He ran twenty feet and then he fell, still clutching the pistol with both hands.

He was dead when Clay knelt beside him. Clay pulled the pistol from his grip and tossed it away. He looked at his own, still in his hand, and then he dropped that too and started down the street. He heard Vanita call to him. He did not look.

In the middle of the street, between the Horseshoe and the Comet, he stopped. "It's over." No one could have heard him. "It's over!" he yelled, raging at them, and raging at himself. "Anse and Barr are dead!"

Tol Shepherd came to stand beside him, repeating Clay's words, calling unseen men by name. Dutch walked from the Horseshoe with a shotgun in his hand.

"For God's sakes, boys!" he called out. "Let's not go any farther with this!" He remembered his shotgun then, and put it hastily on the walk. He came to the middle of the street.

Shepherd was doing all the yelling now.

Three men came from behind the Comet. They still held rifles, but their will to fight had ebbed away. "I never was too strong for this," one said. A few moments later two others joined them on the walk.

Krimble and Wade walked out of the Horseshoe. The Lone Star owner was looking at Clay, and he kept watching Clay all the while Shepherd was going behind the saloon and persuading the hill men there to drop the affair. The townsmen came forth boldly then.

"We can work it out," Shepherd said. "Krimble promised to throw open some of his range."

They had shed each other's blood, Clay thought; and now they would not find it too easy to work out their differences, but that was part of the price they would all have to pay. He walked away suddenly, going up the street.

Chauncey Wade fell in beside him. An impersonal sort of anger ran in Wade's voice. "I want to talk to you about something, Clay."

They walked to where Jeff lay. Doc Covert was just leaving. "There," he said, "was a man with the constitution of a grizzly." He went toward the stable.

Clay took his jumper off.

"Just a minute." Wade's face was grim. "Slaughter, all right. Jeff Slaughter."

Clay spread the jumper and stepped back.

"Did he have two or three old scars around his chest or stomach?" Wade asked.

"Four. One shot broke his hip. You helped do it, Wade."

"That's right, I did." Wade was like a bitter old eagle. "He wasn't your father, Clay. Come over to the hotel with me."

Vanita joined them then. She looked at Clay's face and did not speak.

"Beat it," Wade said. "We got business with your mother."

"I know," Vanita said. "I overheard you and mother that night at Lone Star."

At the door of the hotel Wade said, "By God, you admit it, anyway. Maybe that's something."

Mrs. Krimble was standing at a window, looking down at Bitsy, who was leading Mrs. Honeywell away from a group of men near the doors of Frost's livery.

"She went to Anse first," Mrs. Krimble said. She did not turn around. "I always thought Barr was the favorite, but she went to Anse, and scarcely looked at Barr."

Vanita spoke against a heavy silence. "Mother, Clay is here."

"I saw you in the street." Mrs. Krimble still did not turn. "Are you proud of yourself, Mr. Arbuckle?"

"I didn't kill either of them," Clay said.

"Why not?" Mrs. Krimble turned when there was no answer. "Why not, Mr. Arbuckle?"

"I don't know," Clay said.

"He threw his pistol away afterward," Vanita said. "He walked smack between our side and the others and stopped them from blasting the devil out of each other."

"That is commendable," Mrs. Krimble said. "Your bunkhouse language is not, Vanita." She looked at her daughter with gentle steadiness. "I don't believe you

178

have seen Billy Nairn since we came to town. I suggest that you do so now. Please do not embarrass me by going in the front door of the saloon."

Vanita blushed. She looked at Clay and Wade defensively, and then she left.

Mrs. Krimble sighed. "She has not grown up as fast as I had hoped, in spite of her forward ways." She looked at Clay and then at Wade. "Well, Chauncey?"

Wade sighed. "This is him. To hell—excuse me, Alice—to heck with how it strikes Jim."

"Yes, to hell with it," Mrs. Krimble said. "The use of profanity is occasionally correct. Sit down, Mr.— sit down, both of you." She nodded at Wade when both men were seated on the bed. "Tell it as gently as you can."

Wade cleared his throat. He thought a moment, and then he said, "You're Krimble's son, Clay. Your name is Kevin."

Alice Krimble watched Clay's face all the time Wade unrolled the story.

"She ran off with Jeff Slaughter, Clay. Me and Jim caught up and left Slaughter for dead. You were just a baby then. Jim took her back. She ran off with another man six months later, and that time Jim let her go. She's dead now, Clay, fifteen years this fall. I never had much use for her—" Wade looked at Mrs. Krimble "—except that I was in love with her, like every other man that ever saw her."

After a while, still watching Clay, Mrs. Krimble said, "Go on, Chaunce. I've always known that last thing you said."

"We were pulling out of Texas for good, when you were five," Wade said. "We didn't know then that Slaughter was on our trail. We didn't even know he was

179

alive. We had hard luck one rainy night at the Big Red. The herd stampeded. You were in the wagon, Clay. When we finally got back to it, we couldn't find you.

"I want to tell you right now that Jim said it was maybe just as well. I think he figured there was too much of your mother in you. Maybe he thought—"

"Please contain yourself to what you know, Chaunce," Mrs. Krimble said gently.

"We gave you up for dead, that's all," Wade said. "Slaughter must have come in sometime when we were trying to walk back to the wagon, and found you. What happened after that is up to you to tell, if you want to."

Clay did not want to tell anything. One stranger had been thrust upon him as a father, and now he was dead; and now another man was being thrust upon him as his father. "You're sure—about Jeff?" Clay asked.

"It's Slaughter, if that's what you mean."

"He could have been my father."

"Not unless you're five years younger than you are. When you spun that caster at Lone Star, you stopped everything inside of me. You're Kevin Krimble. Did Jeff ever mention your mother's name?"

"Marta."

Mrs. Krimble and Wade looked at each other. "We are not demanding anything of you, Clay," Mrs. Krimble said. "I thought you should know, and Chauncey finally agreed. The facts need not go beyond the three of us."

Wade said, "Vanita overheard us at the ranch."

Mrs. Krimble compressed her lips. "The four of us then." She leaned toward Clay. "You have nothing to be ashamed of, you know, in being Jim's son."

Events had struck Clay too fast. He wanted time to sort over facts and impressions; he wanted a lot of time

180

to adjust himself to what he had learned. First, he would see how Billy Nairn was, and then he would go to Sash, and there, under the sky, out in the hay, he would decide whether he ever wanted to be called anyone's son again.

Someone knocked. Alice Krimble said, "Come in, please." Jim Krimble entered, carrying a pistol by the barrel. He looked hard at Clay. "This is yours. The last time you forgot it was at Lone Star."

Clay took the pistol. "I didn't forget it today."

"Chaunce," Krimble said, "that was Slaughter." His eyes moved toward Clay again. "How'd you know, Chaunce?"

"I didn't—until I saw him a while ago."

"So you claim to be my son, Arbuckle?"

"Jim!" Mrs. Krimble said. "He did not even—"

"I claim nothing." Clay stood up. "I'm not so sure I'd want to be your son, Krimble."

Krimble scowled. "You think you're salty, huh?"

"I know better—now." Clay bowed to Alice Krimble and walked out.

Wade had already started down the hall but now he waited for Clay. At the top of the stairs he touched Clay's arm and nodded toward the room they had just left.

"Sure, Vanita told me," Krimble was saying. "That's him, Alice. I can see Marta sticking out all over him."

"I can see you in everything about him."

There was a short silence. "There might be something in that," Krimble said. "But don't you and Wade start pushin' him at me!"

"Don't worry, Jim. If there is any pushing, as you call it, you will have to do it yourself. You did not make a very auspicious beginning, I must say. In the future please remember you're dealing with a man who did what all the rest of you—except Ben Wavell—lacked the courage to attempt. You will not be dealing with a child you think you own body and soul because of mere accident of birth."

"Well, by God, Alice! No son of mine is going to tell me what to do!"

Clay tried to go on down the steps. Wade grabbed his arm. Wade was smiling. "Let's hear the rest."

"He won't tell you what to do, Jim, and you had better not tell him what to do."

"Well . . . Think of it, Alice. After all these years I've found my boy!"

"Yes, Jim, you found him."

"I'd better hunt him up and tell him—"

"Not now," Mrs. Krimble said. "Leave him alone."

"He might leave!"

"I don't think so, but you can't stop him."

"What had I better do, Alice?"

"You adopted Texas after the war, Jim, and when you moved again you put a star in the yard to show the world what you thought of Texas. I know you'll find a way to show the world what you think of your son, but first you will have to show him. That's all the advice I know."

Clay and Wade went down the steps. "I enjoyed that plenty," Wade said. "For once I wasn't in the middle."

After Clay talked to Nairn and Covert, he knew Nairn would walk again, perhaps in four months, Covert said.

There was a crowd at the back door of the saloon when Clay got on his horse. Bitsy raised one hand in a small salute, not smiling. Clay touched his hat and nodded. Those who were there to stand close to the man who, they would say later, had killed the Honeywells, saw no more than two unimportant gestures between a man and woman.

Vanita Krimble saw more than that. She bit her lip and went back to Billy Nairn.

Clay and Bitsy looked far deeper into the moment, both knowing that time and life were running with them now.

Clay rode alone from South Fork. The coyote cries were but faint echoes of a past; and when the real ones came again their lostness would be theirs alone and not Clay's.

We hope that you enjoyed reading this
Sagebrush Large Print Western.
If you would like to read more Sagebrush titles,
ask your librarian or contact the Publishers:

United States and Canada

Thomas T. Beeler, *Publisher*
Post Office Box 659
Hampton Falls, New Hampshire 03844-0659
(800) 251-8726

United Kingdom, Eire, and
the Republic of South Africa

Isis Publishing Ltd
7 Centremead
Osney Mead
Oxford OX2 0ES England
(01865) 250333

Australia and New Zealand

Australian Large Print Audio & Video P/L
17 Mohr Street
Tullamarine, Victoria, 3043, Australia
1 800 335 364